Rebecca

Other books by Carol Matas

Lisa
Jesper
Daniel's Story
After the War
The Garden
Greater Than Angels
Cloning Miranda
In My Enemy's House
The Lost Locket
Of Two Minds
More Minds
Out of their Minds
Meeting of Minds
The Burning Time
The Primrose Path
The Freak
Telling
The Race
Sworn Enemies

Rebecca

Carol Matas

Scholastic Canada Ltd.

Scholastic Canada Ltd.
175 Hillmount Rd., Markham, Ontario, Canada L6C 1Z7

Scholastic Inc.
555 Broadway, New York, NY 10012, USA

Scholastic Australia Pty Limited
PO Box 579, Gosford, NSW 2250, Australia

Scholastic New Zealand Ltd.
Private Bag 94407, Greenmount, Auckland, New Zealand

Scholastic Publications Ltd.
Villiers House, Clarendon Avenue, Leamington Spa,
Warwickshire CV32 5PR, UK

Canadian Cataloguing in Publication Data

Matas, Carol, 1949-
Rebecca

ISBN 0-439-98718-0

I. Title.

PS8576.A7994R42 2000 jC813'.54 C00-930911-X
PZ7.M423964Re 2000

6 5 4 3 2 1 Printed in Canada 0 1 2 3 4 5/0

Acknowledgements

I have many people to thank for their help with this book. First of all my mother, who told me how her family was burned off their farm in Saskatchewan and about their subsequent move to Winnipeg. This book is inspired by that story. Next, my Uncle Phil and my Aunt Adele, who are now in their nineties and were able to tell me what it was like to grow up in the North End of Winnipeg at the beginning of the century. And my researcher, Lewis Stubbs, who found me such wonderful reference material, particularly the details of school life and life in the North End.

As always, Perry Nodelman critiqued the manuscript and gave me his usual perceptive comments, which were invaluable. My editor, Diane Kerner, also did a great job helping me to clarify the story. And my husband Per Brask listened chapter by chapter and was full of encouragement.

And finally, thank you to The Manitoba Arts Council, The Canada Council, and The Jewish Foundation of Manitoba. Their grants allowed me to take the time for the extensive research necessary for this project.

For my daughter, Rebecca, and my son, Sam.
And also for my grandparents, Fanny and Sam Churchill.

Chapter One

I refused to leave my room.

Fanny had driven me to distraction all day. She had followed me around, popping up when least expected, nagging, constantly *nudzhing*, "Do you know your lines? Have you memorized everything? Are you sure you've practised enough? Let's go over it one more time!" so that I'd grown more nervous and more insecure by the moment, until I finally decided that even though I knew my lines now I'd be sure to forget them, and perhaps it was best to drop the whole thing. I retreated to my room and wouldn't let anyone in. Since I shared the big room with Fanny, Rose, Sarah, Saide and Leah, they all got angrier and angrier with me. I collected hairbrushes on the bed and each time Fanny tried to open the door I threw one — a very successful way of keeping her out.

The trouble was I was also keeping myself in, and I could smell dinner. My stomach began to growl. I wanted to go down to the kitchen but I couldn't bear to be near Fanny.

Just then Fanny knocked again — this time gently, quite different from the frantic pounding of only a few minutes earlier.

"Rebecca dear, I'm sorry," Fanny called. "It's me that's a nervous wreck and I've tried to pretend I'm not by focussing on you but you'll be wonderful. And they won't blame you if it doesn't go well, they'll blame me because it's my words and that's why I'm going *meshugge*. Please, Rebecca, if you don't come and eat we'll be late and we'll miss the whole thing."

I didn't answer. Let her suffer.

"Please, little *chachem*, it's me that's the idiot, I'm sorry."

Well, I considered, if she's going to call me a wise woman I suppose I might give in. A little.

"But you've made me too nervous to go on!" I called.

The door opened a crack. I decided not to throw another hairbrush — it did sound like she was sincerely apologizing. The door opened a little more. Fanny peeked her face around the corner.

"Just come and eat, Rebecca. See how you feel after. Your mama's made corned beef and cabbage. Your favourite!"

That settled it. I couldn't pass up my favourite dish. "I probably won't be able to eat it," I grumbled. "You've got my stomach in such a twist."

Fanny ran into the room and threw her arms around me in relief. "Yes, you'll eat. And then you'll give a wonderful performance at the concert and you'll forgive your Fanny for being such a *nudnik*."

Papa smiled at me when I took my seat. "Rebecca," he

said, "are you all right? You mustn't be nervous."

"I think this will be my last attempt at acting," I said, shouting a little to be heard over the chattering children.

"Don't say that!" Papa remonstrated, as he helped himself to a healthy portion of the main dish which Mama, along with Aunt Shoshana, was serving. "You can follow in your papa's footsteps."

"I don't think I'm cut out for it, Papa," I objected. "I'd rather sit in my room and read a book."

And, I thought to myself, I'm an ugly duckling. No one wants to see me on stage. It's different for Papa. Mama would tell me that he was the most handsome man in the entire country and that when I grew older I'd be a beauty just like him, but it was hard to believe. I did look exactly like Papa, tall, with thick black wavy hair. He had large blue eyes and mine were brown, but that was the only apparent difference. Except I just looked awkward, whereas — well, Fanny used to giggle as the women in town practically fainted when he walked onto the stage!

Papa loved the stage and had organized a theatre group. Every Sunday night a large number of people would drive to the schoolhouse in Oxbow from the adjoining farms to rehearse a play, or discuss a play. That Sunday night there was going to be a performance of original pieces created by young and old. Fanny was the truly talented one, and she'd written a short monologue about coming to Canada. She'd insisted that it had to be acted by a younger person and that, in fact, she'd written it just for me. Papa and Fanny had kept after me until I'd agreed. But I'm shy and don't like the spotlight. So I was terrified.

I stared at my food and realized that I couldn't eat a bite. But with all the normal *mishegoss* of having twenty-one people in the room, all talking or squabbling or telling jokes, no one noticed my distress. I snuck a look at Fanny. Well, *she* had noticed. She was watching me like a hawk. She made a motion for me to eat. I sighed. I couldn't let her down, I realized. I'd agreed and now I had to go through with it.

Zaida, as usual, sat at the head of the table, while Baba served from the stove. I'd never seen Baba sit down to eat, even though every single meal Zaida would tell her to sit. "Sit, Tema," he'd say, and she'd reply, "In a minute, Joseph." But that was the longest minute in history.

Zaida liked to discuss world events with his two sons-in-law — Papa and Aunt Shoshana's husband, Uncle Morris — and with his older boys, Jacob, Aaron and Isaac. David, at sixteen, had just been included in this group and had moved up from his former place lower down at the table. The men would sit at the top of the table and talk, totally ignoring the chaos around them. I sat in the middle of the table across from Fanny, with my younger brother, Solomon, on one side and my little sister, Leah, on the other. I was in charge of making sure they ate properly and behaved at the table. That had been a problem lately because Leah, at age five, had suddenly decided to save food and feed it to the cats. But the cats needed to be hungry or they wouldn't hunt for mice. I always had to watch her. And Sol was so tenderhearted he'd help her with her little mission of mercy.

After dinner we girls helped to clean up while the boys

hurried out so they could milk the cows, clean the chicken coops, and finish their chores. Then there was the usual fight for water to wash in, whose turn it was, the older ones helping the younger ones — all the time Baba's voice directing everyone: "Rose, you help Saide and Sarah. Aaron, your hands, they're filthy! Where is Ben? Isaac, your shirt is ripped in two places — *oy*, go find another one, do you want to shame me in front of the entire town?"

And Mama calling to us, "Solomon and Leah, hurry up, what slowpokes, just like your papa." And Aunt Shoshana trying to calm her baby, Abe, who was screaming at the top of his lungs.

I managed to pour some water in my washstand and was able to wash up. Normally, since Fanny is seventeen — five years older than I am — I would have to wait while she used the one mirror in our room. But that night she put me in front of it, braided my hair, and helped me dress. I only owned one good white blouse and one good skirt, so the choice of what to wear was simple.

When I was ready I slipped outside to wait for the others. Max and Shmuel were already there. As usual, Shmuel looked neat and handsome, his blond hair neatly combed back with water, while Max looked like a comb had never touched his mop of red hair and his face was already dirty.

I rolled my eyes, and Max shook his head at me. "Don't give your uncle such a disrespectful look!" Max scolded.

"Respect must be earned, dear Uncle Max," I said. "One day you will learn to respect a comb."

Max just loved to tease me about being my uncle. He was thirteen, a year older than me; Shmuel had been born two days after me and he was my uncle too. Mama was the oldest girl of the Churchill family, had married Papa in the Old Country and had had us children even as her own mama, my baba, was still having babies. So twelve of the children were actually my aunts and uncles, right down to Saide, who was only eight! Shoshana and Rose were the only ones I called aunt, though, as they were the oldest. The rest felt more like my brothers and sisters, although it was easy to tell the two families apart — the Churchills were either blond or red-headed whereas we Bernstein children were all dark.

"So, Rebecca," Max said casually, "I suppose you'll get up there and make a complete and utter fool of yourself and the world will come to an end."

My stomach did another flip. "You're right."

"Max!" Shmuel gave him a hard jab with his elbow.

But looking at Max's face, I suddenly realized that he was trying to help me. A bad performance couldn't mean the end of the world, could it? I grinned.

Max noticed my grin, jabbed Shmuel back and said, "No? Not the end of the world? What a relief! I was beginning to think I'd have to repent early — and Yom Kippur weeks away!"

Zaida came out of the house then, Baba behind him hustling all the children with her, Fanny yelling at all of them to hurry or we'd miss everything.

Everyone scrambled into the back of the haywagon. Zaida and Baba got into the small buggy that Jacob had brought around for them. Uncle Morris took the reins of the haywagon. And we set off.

The heat was still overwhelming, even though the sun was dipping lower in the sky. Heat waves lifted off the dry ground, and flies and yellow jackets buzzed around the wagon. The mosquitoes, thankfully, were almost all dead, as it was the beginning of September. Most of the wheat had been harvested, a good crop, and that's why we could relax a little.

I hardly heard the chatter of the others as I concentrated on my speech, rehearsing it over and over in my mind. It was a twenty-minute drive to the school, but to me, my stomach lurching, my heart fluttering, it went by far too slowly, and on the other hand, too quickly.

When we arrived at the two-room schoolhouse, we found all our neighbours and friends going in already, so we had no time for the usual catching up on the week's news. In no time we were all seated. Fanny dragged me to the front of the room and plunked me down beside her on a chair in the first row. Papa and some friends began the show with a short skit about the difficulty of the coming winter, a comedy, but although I could hear the laughter I couldn't hear their words — I was too nervous and all I could do was repeat the words of my piece over and over again. There was boisterous applause when they finished.

I broke out into an awful sweat — it was my turn. Fanny had to push me out of my chair. Slowly, as if in a dream, I walked to the stage, which was a wide wooden platform put up every time we had a concert. I looked out into the semi-darkened room and was able to recognize every face looking expectantly at me. I opened my mouth and to my great surprise, somehow the words came out.

"The year was 1904. And I was four years old when my papa and my zaida boarded up our windows and my mama plugged up my ears with cotton so I wouldn't hear the screaming. I was four years old when my papa explained that bad people wanted to hurt us because we were Jews, but I didn't understand: everyone was a Jew. What was not to like? I was four years old when I crept out of our house after that night of terror and I saw death; and I saw everything around me had been destroyed. I was four years old when my papa and my zaida left to find us a new home.

"I was six years old when we left our home in Odessa, Russia. I was six years old when we got on the ship and the boat rocked and everyone was sick. I was six years old when we got off the boat in Canada and they changed Zaida's name from Chechensky to Churchill, but let Papa keep his name, Bernstein. I was six years old when we got on a train and travelled to the big city, Montreal, and I was still six years old when we got back on the train and travelled to Winnipeg. And we ran up and down the corridors and we looked out at the blue sky and slept on the seats. I was six years old when I came to Oxbow to be part of the Hirsch community and the sky went on forever and the land was hard. I was six years old when Baba said to Zaida, that first winter, "Where have you brought us, Siberia?"

The crowd laughed. I felt a thrill of relief wash through me. It was working!

I opened my mouth to continue when the laughter died down. Only there was one problem — I could no longer remember even one word. My mind was a complete blank. I stared at the audience. They stared at me. Abe squealed. Baba hushed him. My heart thudded in my chest. I could feel the heat rush to my cheeks, and my face must have been turning a bright red. Fanny stood up. She was mouthing something but I couldn't understand what it was. Desperately I racked my brains. I repeated the last line to myself, hoping that perhaps that would remind me, but it didn't help at all. Fanny leaped from her seat and in seconds was standing beside me. She grabbed my hand so I couldn't leave the stage and she began to say the lines. Fanny was speaking to the audience and to me, pretending, I suppose, that this was the way it was supposed to be.

"But now I'm grown up," Fanny said, and suddenly I remembered. Fanny squeezed my hand. I said the next line. "But I sometimes wonder what our lives would have been like if we'd stayed in Odessa." She jumped in with the line after that. Then my turn. And soon it was over. The audience cheered, Max whistled. Fanny pulled me into a bow with her, and then we hurried off the stage.

I sat down in my chair and tried not to cry. I was embarrassed and humiliated. How could I have forgotten everything? I'd known it all by heart. Everyone would hate me. Everyone would think I was an idiot, a *bulbenik.* I stared at my hands. I tried to mutter an apology to Fanny. And then, finally, after what seemed an eternity, the show was over. Papa was the first one over, followed by Mama.

"Rebecca," Papa said, "you were charming."

"Papa!" I objected, "you know that isn't true."

"He's right, darling," Mama agreed. "You were. And no one could tell you forgot. Fanny made it look like it was planned that way."

I knew they were lying but it made me feel a little better. My best friend Masha ran up to me and hugged me.

"You were wonderful," she exclaimed. "You looked so pretty and you spoke so clearly. Why, I understood every word!"

"Masha," I whispered, "I was dreadful! I forgot the words!"

"Oh, that," Masha scoffed. "Who cares about that? You remembered when Fanny got up there with you, and you both spoke beautifully!"

I didn't deserve such kindness. What a failure I'd been. Max and Shmuel came up to us. Max gave me a push.

"Lose your brain?" Max asked.

"She was fine," Shmuel insisted.

"I must have lost my wits," I agreed, thankful that at least Max was telling me the truth.

"So," Max looked around, "has the world come to an end? Should I say my prayers?"

This time his words didn't help. "There's something in between the end of the world and perfection," I snapped. "Total, complete embarrassment. I'm a big *shlemiel.*"

"Yes," Max agreed, "you are. But we knew that already!"

He was determined to make me laugh — it was so annoying!

I hit him on the shoulder. "You're impossible."

"No," Max said, "You are. You're the *shlemiel.*"

"I'm not!" I declared.

"You just said you were!"

"I take it back!"

Soon everyone was talking about the week's news, and

the concert was no longer the only thing under discussion. Finally it was time to leave — not soon enough for me. Although many people had congratulated me I was anxious to get back to my room where I could be miserable in peace — well, as miserable as Fanny and the other girls would let me be.

Once in the wagon I crawled over to Fanny.

"Fanny," I asked, "are you mad?"

"No, of course not," Fanny answered. "People liked it. They liked what I wrote." She seemed thrilled. In fact she spent the rest of the ride home telling me every single comment every single person had made to her about the piece. She was talking so fast and so intensely that at first we didn't hear my papa as he spoke to us. "Shush! Shush! Zaida's calling," he said. "I can't hear what he's saying." Zaida was in the buggy ahead of us.

But then we heard him. And at the same time we saw why he was calling to us.

"Fire!"

I lifted myself up, pushing against the railing of the wagon. And I could see flames ahead.

"Is it the house?" I cried.

"I can't see from here," Papa answered.

"I think it is," Max called. "I think it's the house!"

And then I heard a horrible scream. It was Baba. Actually, the sound was closer to a howl. "No . . . no . . . *no*!"

Chapter Two

The horses were moving too slowly, so all the older children, along with Uncle Morris, leaped off and ran toward the house. Papa turned to me. "Rebecca," he said. "You stay here with the little children."

I grabbed Sarah, who was nine and could easily watch the younger ones. "Sarah, you guard them — don't let them out of your sight. Don't let them off the wagon! I'm going!" I could no more have stayed on that wagon than I could have become a famous actress.

I ran along the dirt road toward my home. I knew that Zaida had just been paid for the crop and that the money was in the house, along with every single thing we owned. Zaida's buggy was well ahead and I could hear Baba's cries wafting back on the wind: "Please God, please God," praying it wasn't as bad as it looked. But as I got closer I could see that the entire house was engulfed in flames and that it had spread to the barn. The animals were shrieking in fear.

"The animals," Morris yelled. "We must get the animals out."

There were seven cows in one barn and two horses in a smaller one. Max, Shmuel and I always fed and groomed the horses so it was natural for us to race for them while the others ran toward the large barn. No one even attempted to go into the house — we could see it was hopeless. The horses were letting out high-pitched sounds of panic and were so wild I had no idea how we were going to get them out. There was smoke in the barn but no fire as yet, so Max and I undid the stall doors and Shmuel slapped their behinds to get them to move. The horses reared up and pawed the air, seemingly unable to move forward, even with the doors open.

"Bridle?" Max screamed over the noise.

I shook my head. "We'll never get them on."

"We'll have to ride them out, then," Max shouted. "I'll try first."

Shmuel yelled, "Look at them Max, you'll never get on their backs. We have to make them leave, push them from behind."

For once I agreed with Shmuel. Max had, as usual, chosen the reckless route but I was sure it wouldn't work. I looked around the barn until my eye fell on a large tin pail. I grabbed one of the pieces of the harness and the pail. "Get up there," I ordered Max. He followed my directions, scrambling onto the wooden slats that separated the two horse stalls. He slid to the back. I threw him the pail, then the harness. Once he was holding them both, he pounded on the pail with the harness. The horses startled even more, but ran forward away from the noise, out into the night. Shmuel and Max and I ran after them.

Outside, all that could be seen was the huge glow of the fire against the small half-circle of orange-red as the sun dipped below the horizon. Three cows were out on the lawn; the others, still in the barn, shrieked in fear and agony.

Zaida was pushing everyone away from the house and the barn.

"That's all we can do," he said. "It's finished. Finished."

"How could it have happened?" Baba wailed.

"Who knows?" Zaida replied, trying to soothe her. "It doesn't matter."

Baba rounded on the children. "Someone left the stove burning. Or a lamp! Who was it?"

Mama had fetched the younger children from the wagon, and they were crying already. This made them cry harder. Abe began to wail in Aunt Shoshana's arms. Leah began to howl and Sarah and Saide joined in. I knew Baba's temper too well, as did all the children, and we quickly realized that someone would be blamed — nothing bad could happen without Baba blaming it on someone. If there was no person obviously responsible, she blamed God.

"Baba's right for once," I muttered to Max. "Someone did something stupid and now look! What's going to happen?"

As usual Shmuel was beside Max and me. "Rebecca," he chastised me, "do you really want to find someone to blame? It could've been you that tipped a lamp when you were rushing to get ready."

My heart sank. Had it been me? Had I done something that stupid?

Shmuel saw the look of dismay on my face. "You see," he said, "it doesn't help." He paused and shook his head, and I noticed there was a tear trickling down his cheek.

Max backed us farther away from the house, now an inferno of heat, flames and the crackling of wood. Zaida was calling us. "Children! I want all the children by me. Is everyone here?"

He counted heads and found that all were safe. Three cows, five horses, a buggy, and the haywagon were now everything we had left in the world.

Neighbours from other farms began to arrive. They had seen the flames — easy to spot across the open flat prairie. But they soon saw there was nothing to be done except to make sure the fire was contained and to see that it didn't spread to the brush or the trees. We children huddled together and shivered in the cool night air as we watched, completely helpless. I don't know how long it was, but finally the fire burned itself out.

"Tie the animals to the wagon," Zaida ordered, when he was satisfied that it was safe to leave. "We need a place to sleep. We'll go back to town to the schoolhouse for the night. Mendel Jacovitch will help us."

Mr. Jacovitch ran the General Store in Oxbow and his place was where everyone gathered for information, food, and supplies. Fanny and I retrieved a length of rope from the wagon so the older boys could tie up the animals — not an easy task since the poor beasts were so jumpy. The neighbours gave their condolences and returned home.

It was dark as our family slowly made our way back to town, the dirt road lit only by the remnants of the fire behind us and the moon just rising up in the sky. The children wept inconsolably or sniffled, the adults spoke quietly amongst themselves, trying to appear calm and brave. But everyone knew that here was a complete disaster.

I began to panic as the extent of the calamity sank in. We were destitute. Where could we live? Where would we go? I wriggled over to Mama and began to ask her what would happen but Mama only said, "Rebecca, you must help me with Sol and Leah. You're their big sister. You must be brave." So I had to calm little Leah, and Sol, who was always timid, was trembling so hard I had to try to soothe him as well. I wanted to scream, what about me? I'm scared too! But as the oldest, I couldn't. I noticed that Fanny was in the same boat, comforting her younger brothers and sisters, even though she must have been terrified herself.

When we finally reached town we dragged ourselves into the large Jacovitch kitchen.

"What has happened?" Mrs. Jacovitch cried when she saw us. Her white hair was loose down her back and she had wrapped herself in a white robe.

"Our house," Baba moaned, "gone in smoke. Gone!"

"*Oy, oy gevalt!*" Mrs. Jacovitch exclaimed. "Under no circumstances can a person ensure himself of anything!"

Mr. Jacovitch had dressed quickly and his hair was sticking straight up. He shook his head. "In the Torah, Job warns us, " 'Man is born unto trouble, as the sparks fly upward.' "

At the mention of sparks the younger children began to cry again.

Mrs. Jacovitch slapped Mr. Jacovitch, "Mendel," she chastised him, "you are a *shtunk*!"

That turned some of the tears into giggles. Mrs. Jacovitch made some hot milk and insisted we drink it before trying to sleep. I felt a little comforted as it warmed me. We settled the younger children on the floor. The adults stayed at the Jacovitches' with the little ones, while Rose, Jacob, Fanny, Aaron, Isaac, David, Max, Shmuel, and I went to the schoolhouse. We sat on blankets on the floor of the larger room, where the performances had been only hours earlier. We were all silent until Fanny spoke.

"There's no money," she said, stating the obvious. "And nowhere to live. I think we'll have to leave and go to a town or a city."

"We can build another house before winter," Jacob objected. "We shouldn't leave!"

Aunt Rose, who was always calm and wise, spoke quietly. "It's not for us to say. Papa will decide what's best. He'll think of all sides, and then he'll make up his mind. Now I want everyone to try to get a little sleep. Morning will be here soon enough and we'll need our strength to help Papa and Mama and to look after the little ones."

I was suddenly exhausted. I lay down on my blanket, and fell asleep quickly — perhaps as a way to escape my new circumstances.

When I awoke the next morning, at first I really had no

idea where I was or what had happened. I looked around and saw the others beginning to sit up, rubbing their eyes, as if they too were confused. Without a word we all slowly got up and made our way to the Jacovitches' house.

There, Mr. Jacovitch greeted us. "Ah, children," he said, shaking his head as we trooped into the kitchen, "If it doesn't get better, depend on it, it will get worse."

Mrs. Jacovitch scolded him. "A fool grows without rain!"

Baba, Mama, and Shoshana were already feeding the little children.

"The men have gone to sell the animals," Baba told us. "We are going to Winnipeg to live. I hope that whoever caused this accident can live with themselves!"

"Mama," my mama said, "Please, what good does this kind of talk do? You don't think the children are upset enough?"

"If they thought first," Baba answered, "they wouldn't get upset later."

Mama rolled her eyes. "Come and eat," she urged us. "We don't need anyone getting sick or weak."

We managed some oatmeal and then we all wanted to go see our friends. Mama told me I could leave, so I ran to find Masha. In fact, because our family made up so much of the schoolroom, and since all our friends wanted to see us, Miss George suspended school for the day. Masha and I walked down the main street.

"I thought this summer's storm was the most frightening thing I would have to live through," I said.

"Me too," Masha agreed. A cyclone had torn through

the prairie, almost pulling the roof off our house, and destroying many buildings in nearby Estevan.

"But this is much worse," I continued. "I'll be separated from you and everyone here and I'll have to be in a new school where I don't know anyone."

Masha nodded her head sympathetically. We were the two shyest girls in the community and had found each other because, outside of our families, we felt it so hard to be comfortable around others.

"What if everyone hates me?" I asked. "What if they think I'm an ugly good-for-nothing?"

"You just have to give them time to get to know you," Masha said. "But it'll be hard for me too, having you leave. At least you won't have to put up with Miss George any more," she added.

"I don't understand why a person who hates Jewish people would accept a post at a school with only Jewish children," I remarked.

"She probably had no choice," Masha speculated. "Perhaps she had to do what the government told her to do."

"It would be nice to have a better teacher," I agreed. "But that could never make up for leaving here." I felt tears burning at my eyes.

"Now, Rebecca Bernstein," Masha rebuked me, "don't you start crying. If you start, I'll start and I simply won't be able to stop!"

She was right, so I fought back the tears. "Do you remember," I asked, trying to think of a way to lighten the moment, "the time Max convinced us to pretend to be ghosts and *dybbuks* on Purim? And how scared the little children were in school that day?"

She giggled. "I can't believe we did that."

"Neither could Miss George," I said. "'I cannot believe it of you two girls,'" I mimicked her. "'You are always my best-behaved young ladies.'"

"Max can make you do anything," Masha smiled. She sighed. "I'll miss him, too. I have an idea," she said. "Let's walk through the town and try to remember everything that happened at each different spot."

"For instance," I suggested, "when we pass the Washenskis' store we can remember how we both were sick all night when we ate almost a pound of lemon drops, because they were so good and we'd never tasted anything like them and we couldn't stop."

"Or when we pass the post office we can think about how we sent that letter to Mr. Frank Baum, telling him how much we love his Oz books."

We spent the rest of the day walking through the town, reminiscing about the six years we had known each other and wandering into the stores, saying goodbye to everyone. When it was time to say goodbye to each other we had run out of words. We threw our arms around each other and our resolve not to cry was forgotten — we wept.

That night my family was quiet as we all lay down on our blankets, and even Max didn't have any smart remarks.

The next morning we boarded the train to Winnipeg.

"'Don't worry about tomorrow, who knows what will happen to you today,'" Zaida said, loud enough for us all to hear as we settled into our seats. It was his favourite saying from the Talmud and he repeated it almost daily. There was a lot of truth to it, I thought. "Remember," he continued, "if God does not approve, a fly won't make a move."

Papa sat down beside me. I turned to him. "Is it true, do you think, Papa? Did God mean this to happen to us for a reason?"

"Rebecca," Papa admonished me, "you know I don't believe that. I'm a free thinker! All this religious talk is nonsense, pure and simple! What happened was a bad accident, that's all."

I sighed inwardly. Zaida's philosophy was much more comforting than Papa's, and I needed comforting. I knew that Mama agreed with Papa, but since I'd grown up with both views, I really never knew which one was right. One day I believed that God was in charge of my destiny; the next day, I had to allow that God was just a figment of the world's imagination.

Maybe it was thinking about imagination that made me suddenly remember that amongst my clothes and dolls and all my belongings, my books had burned too — the ones I'd borrowed from the big library in Estevan.

"Papa," I wailed, "all my beautiful books. They're gone!"

"Your books?" He paused for a minute to think. "I will write the library and explain what has happened. And once in Winnipeg we can join the library there and you can borrow them again. Who knows, perhaps we'll be so rich in Winnipeg you could own one! Now, what would Dorothy from Kansas do in this situation? Cry? I don't think so!"

He was right, of course. Dorothy never cried or gave up. She was far too brave and adventurous. Everything was an adventure for Dorothy.

Well, it could be for me too, I thought. It could be an adventure instead of a disaster. But I didn't really believe it. Inside I was quaking with fear.

Chapter Three

I stared out the window as the train chugged along and thought back to our time in the Hirsch colony. We'd had everything we needed there: a school, a synagogue, three stores, a blacksmith. All the Jewish farmers in the colony were like one big family. My family had struggled so hard to make a good farm. We had worked together and worked hard. One year, locusts had destroyed our crop; another year, it was destroyed by drought. Through every one of those difficulties Zaida had never given up. This past summer the cyclone had somehow spared our farm and we'd thought ourselves very fortunate. But now it seemed that losing all our money was a disaster that was too great to overcome.

I couldn't help but think back to the house that was now nothing but ashes. The farmstead had started as a one-room log hut. Every summer the men had added to it, until it was a large home with two floors and lots of room and a dirt cellar where Baba kept her barrels of pickles and sauerkraut in the winter. We had been planning to pickle the small round watermelons from the garden, and in a couple of weeks it would have been the tomatoes. The apples were ripe now too, ready for picking. I missed my room, I missed the cool dark cellar, I missed the kitchen where we would eat and talk and laugh.

Max, seated across the aisle, interrupted my musings. "Worried?"

"Aren't you?"

"Me? I'm excited! The big city! I can't wait. And the school will be better. Bound to be."

Max was a brilliant student. He'd had a lot of trouble with Miss George who never challenged him in his work because she assumed he was stupid. She assumed that about all of us, but it had bothered Max the most, because he would get so bored — and then get into trouble, of course!

"I'll be glad to go to a different school," Max continued. "Hopefully we'll have smart, big-city teachers and we'll be taught properly, like everyone else."

My stomach lurched. Strangers. Bunches of them. Still, Shmuel and I were the same age. Maybe we'd be in the same class. That was something to grasp on to.

"But where will we live?" I asked, voicing my biggest fear.

Max reached across the aisle and gave me a little shove. "They have houses in Winnipeg! That's what a city is," he said, teasing me. "Lots of houses, all in the same area!" He paused and his eyes shone with excitement. "They have stores of all kinds, wait till you see, it'll be wonderful. I've been told that there's even a store filled to the rim only with books!"

"Really?"

"Really."

Well, maybe the big city wouldn't be so bad after all. And they would have lending libraries too, like in Estevan, only bigger. Whatever happened I would always have books to read.

The chug of the train, the gentle sway, and the fatigue of the last few days finally caught up with me and I dropped off to sleep, only to be woken by the conductor calling out, "Winnipeg! Winnipeg next!"

We got off the train at the CPR station, Baba shouting orders, the children crying from being rudely awakened. I found Mama and shrank next to her, keeping a firm grip on Leah with one hand, Solomon with the other.

People accosted us the moment we entered the station. It was pandemonium.

"Need a place to stay? Come with me," said a little man with greasy hair, wearing a filthy black suit.

"No, don't listen to him. He's not one of us. Listen to me," said a tall lanky man. "I'm a landsman. Like you. You'll come with me. For a small fee, I find you a place to stay, I help you out."

Another was grabbing at Zaida's coat. "You don't want nothing to do with those *no-goodniks.* You stick with me. I find you a place to stay. You need a place?"

I looked at Zaida. Surely he had a place. Didn't he? And then much to my dismay, he seemed to choose one of the men, told all of us to wait, and off he went.

That wait, the hours in that station, were the worst hours of my life — up until that point, that is. The noise. The screaming. The chaos. There were peddlers everywhere hawking one thing or another — fruit, big twisted pretzels, watches, everything. And where was Papa? He, too, had disappeared. When I finally spotted him wading through the crowds of people, I almost wept with relief. And then came the bad news.

He spoke to Mama. "Your father can only find a house big enough for them. An extra five bodies, they can't fit in. Not yet. We need a little room of our own. I've paid a man who gave me this address. He says it's very nice. One big room. It's on," he looked at the paper, "Jarvis Street."

"You paid him already?" Mama asked.

"Why not?"

I wondered why not as well? Why was Mama worried about *that*? We were to be separated from the rest of the family! *That* was what she should have been worried about! How was I to manage without Max and Shmuel? I'd never spent a second away from them. How could Papa say so casually that there was no room for us in Zaida's house, as if it didn't matter?

"Papa," I began to object, but he cut me off.

"Rebecca, help your mama with the bags. We need to hurry. I can't wait to see it."

We had almost no bags since everything had been destroyed in the fire, but I helped with what little we had and followed Papa outside of the station. And once outside I forgot all my worries temporarily, because I was so overwhelmed by what I saw. There were so many buildings! And they were so large!

In front of us was a wide mud road. Horse-drawn buggies trotted past us, people rode bicycles, shiny automobiles chugged along. The sidewalk was packed with people dressed in everything from rags to the most exquisite finery. Leah held Mama's hand and Sol held Papa's and I trailed after them, eyes wide in wonder. We passed the Royal Alexander hotel, which I thought at first must be a palace. Outside its grand front doors, men in brilliant livery helped ladies out of buggies, and reached down to help men out of their roadsters. The men wore silk scarves draped around their necks and carried walking sticks with gold handles!

We walked under the train overpass and continued north down Main Street. We passed a restaurant called Boston, a much smaller hotel called the Sutherland, a jeweller, a tinsmith, a laundry, a baker, a general store. "It's so big," I whispered.

"Yes," said Papa, eyes sparkling. "But think, Rebecca. They have real theatres here. Perhaps I can act in plays on a real stage."

Mama let out a sigh. "First you need a paying job, Simon," she reminded him. "We're on our own now."

Papa looked serious then. "Of course we are. But don't worry, Miriam. We'll manage. You'll see."

"Do you have Zaida's address?" I asked, my worry about being separated from the rest of the family for even a moment returning.

"Of course I do," Papa answered. "He's only a couple of

blocks over, on Selkirk Avenue. Don't worry."

When we finally reached Jarvis Street, we found ourselves on a narrow mud road. On either side were tall rows of houses, all joined together. A sidewalk made of boards ran between them. Papa searched for the house number. We followed him, the boards creaking under our feet. Papa found the number and knocked on the door. An old man answered. He was dressed in rags and his front teeth were missing. He spoke Yiddish to us.

"*Nu?*"

"We're here about the room," Papa said.

"Ah, of course, you follow me." He didn't ask us our names, or shake hands, or do any of the things I had come to expect when strangers met in Oxbow. It was so dark in the front room I couldn't really see anything. I followed Papa and Mama through a door just off the front room.

"I can't see anything," Papa complained. "Could we have a lamp please?"

The man grunted, then shuffled away. We stood there helplessly, unable to even see if there was a window to open, it was so dark. Finally the man returned with a lamp. He held it up.

"Okay?" he asked.

Papa and Mama looked around. It was a small room, barely large enough for two people. Papa found the window. It was covered in dirt, letting in almost no light, so he opened it. Finally, with the light from the window and the lamp, we could see more clearly. Leah and Sol shrieked and so did I. The walls, which had at first seemed black, perhaps from dirt, were moving. They were covered, every inch, with bugs, huge bugs.

"What is that?" Papa exclaimed.

"*Ach*, just the cockroaches. You can poison them if you want," the man said.

I turned, pulling Leah and Sol with me, and ran. And so did my parents. We stood on the wooden platform gasping for breath. I felt sure the huge bugs were crawling all over me. I rubbed my hair, brushed my clothes, kicked my feet. There was one on my boot! I brushed it off with a squeal. Sol stomped on it.

"Now what, Simon?" Mama said, as she checked us all over. "Now what?"

"We'll go to Selkirk Avenue and find your father," Papa said. "What else can we do?"

Chapter Four

Selkirk Avenue. I forgot all about the bugs as I looked around in wonder. I noticed that the street was paved with shaved blocks of wood, unlike the mud of the other streets we had crossed on the way. And there were people everywhere. Friendly people, saying hello in Yiddish, in Russian, in Ukrainian, just as they did back home. We passed a hardware store, a tailor shop, then a dry goods store, a pool hall, a kosher butcher, another hardware store, a baker, a movie theatre, a furniture store, *another* movie theatre, a photographer's shop, a barbershop, and too many small grocers and delicatessens to count. I wanted to go in and explore each and every one. Papa had to keep calling me to keep up, as I dragged behind the rest of them. Before I knew it we were at the address Papa had — it was an empty storefront and through the front pane of glass I could see Max! I ran in and threw my arms around him. He grinned.

"It's only been two hours since I last saw you, Rebecca.

Can't you manage on your own for even that long?"

I was so elated seeing my entire *mishpocheh* that I almost felt faint. My family, my clan, they were all there — Baba coming down the stairs, her voice loud, "This is a home? This is a house? *Oy. Oy.* Well, it could be worse. We'll manage."

"We're going to make a store here," Max told me. "A butcher shop, non-kosher. There's already a kosher butcher right near here and Papa doesn't want to compete with them. We can buy the meat from them that our family will eat — Mama says she's always had a kosher home and she won't stop now. Funny, huh? We won't be able to eat our own meat! But this way Papa feels we can sell to Jews who don't keep kosher and to everyone else around here. And that's lots of people," he added.

Shmuel came in from another room. "Rebecca! Have you found a good place?"

Mama burst into tears. Baba went over to her. "What? What?"

Papa hung his head. "It's my fault, Mama. I met this man, he seemed like a real gentleman. I paid him money for a room but it was no good."

"No good," muttered Mama through her tears. "He was nothing but a *draykop.*"

"It was covered in bugs!" I added. "I mean *covered.* There must have been thousands in that one room!"

"Like the one crawling in your hair?" Max asked innocently.

I shrieked and started to jump around, almost pulling my braid apart in a frenzy, trying to get the horrible cockroach out.

Shmuel kicked Max. "Rebecca, there's nothing there. He's teasing."

"Are you sure?" I asked, still brushing frantically at my head.

Shmuel stood on his toes for an inspection. "Nothing."

I glared at Max. "You *bulvon*!" I cried.

"I'm insulted," Max retorted, putting a hurt look on his face, but he was still laughing at my panic over the bug. To be called a blockhead by me was nothing new to Max. I called him that all the time. *Bulvon* had practically become my pet name for him.

Baba gave Mama a hug. "Don't worry, darling. You'll stay with us until you find another place." She shot Papa an evil look as if she were blaming him. "Somehow, God willing, we'll manage."

Zaida had been quietly watching as they talked. "Now," he said, "let me remind all of you — God's will may have brought us here but we have to make our own *mazel*. We can't expect Him to do everything."

I wondered if that were true. After all, luck, or *mazel*, was just that wasn't it? Luck? Could you make your own? Or did you just have to live with the luck you got? Or didn't get?

Zaida was busy making his now. "I'm going to speak to our new neighbours. I know that there are societies, loan societies that will help us to get a start. No time to waste." And he hurried off.

Then Baba took control. "Children, we need mats to sleep on; beds will come later. Max, Fanny, Shmuel, go and find us what to sleep on. Jacob, Rose, you go find us cheap pots and pans and plates. Isaac, David, Aaron, we need a kitchen table and we need chairs." She began to hand out money to the leader of each group. "Nothing fancy, mind," she chided. "Just enough to get us going. But clean! No bugs, right Rebecca?"

I managed a weak smile and then happily trudged off after my cousins. I didn't care how meagre the surroundings were. I was just glad to be back with my *mishpocheh.*

I took Fanny's hand. Fanny had barely spoken a word since I'd arrived.

"Why are you so quiet?" I asked her as we walked out into the street.

"I'm memorizing all my first impressions," Fanny explained, "so I can write a play about my first day in Winnipeg. Your bug experience is excellent."

I rolled my eyes. "I'm delighted to supply you with such good material," I said.

Max and Shmuel were quickly getting lost in the crowd ahead. Fanny and I hurried after them to find them peering into the window of a used furniture store. Aaron, Isaac and David arrived soon after.

"Who's our best negotiator?" Fanny asked.

We all looked at Max.

"Fine," he agreed. "I'll do it."

"We'll choose everything," Aaron said. "Then you bargain."

In no time we had found mattresses, a table, and chairs and it was left up to Max to come to a price with Mr. Tannenbaum, the owner. Back and forth, back and forth they went until the money was agreed upon and we began to *shlep* it all back down the street. I didn't mind the work, though. I was so relieved to be away from the room on Jarvis Street that I didn't think I'd ever mind anything again.

While we'd been gone Mama and Aunt Shoshana had been to the stores and had returned with bread, apples and some cheese. Once the table was set up in the kitchen and the stove fired, Baba boiled water in a huge cauldron, then put all the new plates and cutlery in it. Mama cut up the bread and the small children were fed. We were all faint from hunger and gobbled down the food as soon as we were allowed to eat.

Zaida returned. "I've been given a loan," he announced. "The Hebrew Sick Benefit Society is giving me an interest-free loan to get started. Tomorrow I buy a cow. Then we slaughter it. And then we're in business!"

Max showed me around their new home. The little storefront had one large room facing the street. In the back to the right was the kitchen, on the left was another room, upstairs two more. And, of course, the outhouse was in the back. After the tour, which took only minutes, I realized why Zaida had said that there was not enough room for more than his family of thirteen and why he wanted the two married daughters to find somewhere else to live. Plus, a small butcher shop would be lucky to support Zaida, Baba and the older boys as workers. My papa would have to find another job. So would Uncle Morris.

Uncle Morris actually had training as a tailor, but Papa — he'd been a bit of a failure at everything in the Old Country. At least that's what Baba said. Everyone agreed he was a talented actor and a nice person, but a little hopeless. He'd done fine on the farm, doing chores, working in the fields, building onto the house. But now what?

That first night in Winnipeg I kept rolling off the narrow mattress I shared with Fanny. Finally I wrapped myself in a blanket, also newly bought, and slept right on the hard wood floor. I was so exhausted from all the strangeness and upheaval that I slept well. One thought disturbed me though — the fear of being separated from my cousins. I hoped that somehow Zaida or Papa would find a way to keep us together.

The next morning Baba put us all to work cleaning. We scrubbed every inch of the little house, while Aunt Rose and Fanny cooked a pot of vegetable stew and tried to keep the youngsters out of trouble. New neighbours came in and introduced themselves, but there were so many new faces I couldn't keep any of them straight.

At the end of the day Papa came home, shaking his head, muttering "No luck, no luck." No luck finding work or a place for us to stay. I was relieved about the place, but worried about the work.

The next few days passed in a blur of cleaning, organizing, and if we could get away for a few minutes at a time, exploring. Right next door was a small grocers, run by a Jewish family, the Myersons. One wall was lined with drawers containing sugar, salt, rice, raisins, currants and tea. Cookies and crackers filled barrels along another wall, and glass jars lined up against another held candies. Mrs. Myerson, a tall, plump woman, would meticulously weigh the required items in a small brown bag. On the farm we had made our own soap, but in the Myersons' store it came in a huge blocks and she would slice off chunks for her customers. The boys loved to visit the hardware store down the street; I found a small store that sold books, records and cigars and I'd slip in there whenever I could.

It was our third night in Winnipeg and we were all sitting down to dinner together when Zaida asked us to be quiet. The usual dinner racket was well under way, so it was a few moments before Zaida could speak. Before he even opened his mouth, Mama started to cry. Instead of running over to comfort her or to ask her what the matter was, Papa sat like a stone, staring at the table. My stomach sank and a nasty feeling of foreboding crept over me. What had happened? What was wrong?

"This is our situation," Zaida said. "We have a loan which will help us to get started. But for the first few months things will be very tight. We haven't got room for everyone here, that's obvious. There are other rooms we could rent on this street, but we cannot afford them right now.

"We have cousins, Benjamin and his wife Jenny, who can put Miriam and Simon up. They have one small bed." Mama cried harder at this point, and Aunt Shoshana joined in.

"Morris has found a job at Kay's factory as a tailor and he and Shoshana will rent a room a few blocks over. But Simon hasn't been able to find anything yet. Of course, he will soon. But the problem is that in the meantime we don't have the money to feed everyone. So, we've had to make some difficult choices." He paused here as if uncertain how to go on. Baba sighed a deep sigh.

He turned to me. I held my breath. What could it be?

"Rebecca, you and Sol and Leah must be put in the care of the Hebrew Sick Benefit. They've told me they can find you a nice clean home where you'll have your own bed and you'll be fed properly. You'll go to school. That way you don't have to leave school to work, which would be the worst solution. The older boys are getting jobs on the railroad and we hope your papa can too, Rebecca. This is only temporary. Until we're on our feet."

I didn't understand. Why couldn't I just continue as before? I'd happily sleep on the floor. I wouldn't eat. Not anything. Well, hardly anything. I just didn't want to be sent away!

Surely Mama and Papa won't let this happen, I thought. They know how shy I am, how I hate new things and strangers. Why can't Papa find work? Everyone else can. But the words that were racing through my head wouldn't come out of my mouth. The sight of my mama's tears and my papa's humiliation left me unable to utter a word, as if a huge lump of coal had become stuck in my throat, trapping the words inside.

Finally Papa spoke. Very quietly he said, "I'll get work, Rebecca, I will. And I'll find a place for us. I promise. But there are five of us. It's easier for Morris. They only need one small room for the three of them. We'll need more."

"Why?" I said, somehow finding my voice, although it came out sounding more like a croak than normal speech. "We could live in one room."

"Your mama deserves better," he said. "And anyway, I

don't have enough yet for even one room. Morris has training . . . I don't."

No one spoke. You could have heard a pin drop.

"No," I pleaded. "No."

"Be a big girl, Rebecca," Baba said, her face stern. But I was sure I saw her eyes fill up with tears. "You must set an example for the little ones." She nodded at Solomon and Leah.

I felt that everything had just turned upside-down. Were Baba and Zaida mean and cruel people after all? How could they turn their own grandchildren out? Why would they think it was better for us? For a bed? For food? I'd rather starve. I looked at Leah. I was sure Leah would rather starve too.

"We'd rather starve," I declared, the words finally spilling out. "We'd rather starve and sleep on the floor. But you don't care about us, so, so, I don't want to be here. I don't belong here, do I?" And I got up from the table and ran upstairs.

Chapter Five

I had visits from everyone over the next few hours. My mama sat with me and tried to explain. So did my papa. So did my zaida. But it was Shmuel, walking with me down Selkirk Avenue the next morning, who told me the truth.

"Have you been hungry the last few days, Rebecca?" he asked as we stopped to gaze at fresh apples in a basket outside the grocer's.

I nodded.

"So have I. Have you thought at all about why we're so hungry?"

I shook my head. I hadn't. All I really cared about was being with the family. I'd ignored my growling stomach — it hadn't been important.

"We're hungry because there isn't enough food to go around," Shmuel said quietly. "That's why. If you and your family go and Shoshana and her family go that's the difference of eight mouths to feed. Eight extra mouths, that's a lot."

"But I'll get a job then," I protested. "I can work! I'll bring in money."

"That's exactly what your parents and my parents don't want. They want all of us to finish our education, so we can get good jobs after high school. They want us boys to go on to university. They'd rather sacrifice now so that can happen. Anyway, we'll all have to work in the store after school. Rebecca, it's only for a little while until your papa gets on his feet. He'll get a job and he'll save enough for a nice place. You'll see."

I sighed. I had to accept it, I could see that now. They were only doing what they thought was best for me. A bed to sleep in, food on the table, and going to school instead of going to work.

"School's already begun," Shmuel said. "Mama says we'll all start together on Tuesday. She'll let Shmuel and me wait for you so you don't have to start alone. You're to go to the new place tomorrow. But not until the afternoon. Apparently on Monday the mother volunteers at their church."

"Church?" I turned and stared at him. "What do you mean?"

"Didn't anyone tell you?"

"Tell me what?"

He bit his lip. "I thought they'd told you."

"What?"

"Solomon and Leah are going together to an observant Jewish home only a few blocks away, but they had no room for three. There just aren't enough Jewish foster homes — in fact the community is building a Jewish orphanage just for that reason, but it won't be ready for a year or more. So . . ." he paused, then spit it out. "You aren't going to a Jewish home. They couldn't find one for you. The Hebrew Sick found you a home with a Ukrainian family. Very religious. They believe it's their duty to help. That's what Papa told me."

"Why didn't anyone tell *me*?" I exclaimed. I felt even more betrayed, if that were possible.

"I suppose they were going to," Shmuel muttered. "I thought they had. They were probably waiting for the right moment."

I had thought I couldn't feel worse, but now I did. To be torn from my family was bad enough, but I'd assumed I'd be going to a Jewish home where everything would be familiar. They would have Shabbat dinner with fish and chicken, they would know everyone my family knew, it would be the same world. But a non-Jewish family? *Goyish.* Ukrainian? Many Ukrainians in the Old Country hated Jews. What if they were asking me there only to be mean to me just because I was Jewish. And how would I even understand them? I couldn't speak Ukrainian.

I started to cry. People on the street came over, asked Shmuel what was the matter. It was embarrassing, but I kept crying. I couldn't stop.

Shmuel took me by the hand and pulled me back into the house. In the storefront there was already a huge butcher's block. Meat dangled from hooks and was laid out in a cabinet. A woman was berating Zaida, demanding his best chicken, telling him he'd better not be selling her one that wasn't absolutely fresh. My cries had turned to loud hiccups and gasps, and I couldn't catch my breath. Shmuel pulled me into the back room. Fanny happened to be there, looking after the little ones.

"Rebecca," Fanny exclaimed, "you poor thing."

I cried myself out in Fanny's arms. Fanny kept telling me that everything would be all right, but I didn't believe her. I was terrified. A new home. What if they didn't like me? A new school. What if everyone hated me? How could this be happening?

That night I was in a state. I was furious with my parents and my grandparents, anguished over leaving, and terrified that the new family wouldn't like me. I insisted on Papa heating water in a basin for me and I washed every bit of myself, even my hair, with a huge bar of Sunlight soap. I didn't want the new family to think I was dirty. When it was time for sleep I couldn't sleep at all. I lay on the hard floor all night, shivering with fear and dread.

The next morning, I felt like I was in some kind of a dream. None of it seemed real. I said goodbye, no longer feeling any emotion at all, and followed Mama and Papa to my new home on Stella Avenue. I wore my clean white blouse. My hair was braided neatly down one side. The weather was still warm for September so I had a sweater over my blouse, but no jacket. Papa carried my suitcase, Mama held my hand. I had nothing to say to them.

There was a brisk wind and perhaps being outdoors made me realize that I was not in a dream, but that what was happening was all too real. I became angrier and angrier with each step. Maybe it wasn't fair to be angry, but I didn't care. How could they give away their children? I wondered if I would ever feel the same way about Papa again. Why couldn't he get work right away? Was it possible that he *was* just a handsome, nice *shlemiel*? I could barely bring myself to believe such a thing, to even think it, but what else was I to think? He seemed to believe that all sorts of jobs were not good enough for him. Why couldn't he work on the railroad like the other men? He was tall. He was strong.

Stella Avenue wasn't too far from Selkirk Avenue, only two blocks. The street was filled with two-storey houses built close together, wooden sidewalks out front, an unpaved street a few feet below. When we were almost there Papa spoke, as if reading my thoughts.

"Rebecca," he said, "you must believe me, it won't be for long. I promise. But if I take a job doing something I hate I may be stuck in that job forever. I wouldn't have the opportunity, would I, to look for something better. I just need some time to find my feet, that's all."

"But you haven't even been looking, Papa," I exclaimed.

"Yes, of course I have. I've been meeting people and talking to them. That's how you find a good job. That's how you get hired."

I noticed Mama biting her lip. I could see that Mama didn't want to contradict Papa in front of me, but that she obviously had a different opinion.

"Rebecca, I think *I* may have found a job," Mama said then. "At Hershfield's store. Only a few hours a day he could give me, but it's something. A start. You'll see. In no time we'll all be back together."

We had gotten to the address and the three of us stood outside looking at the house.

"What about the New Year?" I asked. "What will happen on Rosh Hashanah? Will you come get me?"

"We'll all go to Baba's, of course, for the first night," Mama assured me. "And that's only a week away! So, you see, it won't be so bad. One week. And you're only a couple of blocks from everyone."

"Everyone except you," I accused them.

"I know we're far away," Mama said, tears in her eyes, "but it was the only place we could go. We'll see you for sure next week. Maybe before. If Papa still has no work, he can come and check on you. How's that?"

I nodded mutely. My stomach was in such a twist I could barely stand. I was trying desperately not to cry. I wanted to make a good first impression so they'd be nice to me, these strangers.

"Come on," Papa said, gently. "Let's go meet them." And he led the way up the three stairs to the door and knocked. No one answered. He knocked again, loudly. I swayed a little, feeling quite dizzy. And the door opened.

Chapter Six

A woman answered the door. She was very short and very round. She had pink cheeks and a babushka wrapped tightly around her hair. She smiled and said something in Ukrainian, waving us inside. Papa had learned some Ukrainian from dealing with our Ukrainian neighbours in Saskatchewan and now he nodded and smiled and said a few words in reply. He turned to me. "This is Mrs. Kostaniuk," he said. "She's really thrilled to have you here, Rebecca. She says she has a daughter, Sophie, just your age and she knows you'll be best friends."

I nodded, and attempted to smile at her, but was unable to. I looked around. The house seemed quite nice. Clean. And Mrs. Kostaniuk seemed friendly, although how I was to understand her I had no idea. The woman chattered on to Papa, who translated for me.

"The children will be home shortly. Sophie is at school, as is her older brother Sasha. There are two other brothers, Vladimir and Piotr, they both work. Will you be all right?"

I nodded again, unable to trust myself to speak for fear of saying something awful or bursting into tears. Mrs. Kostaniuk offered Mama and Papa tea, but they refused and moved awkwardly to the door. They all shook hands and smiled, Papa turning abruptly and stalking out as if the shame of what was happening had just struck him. Mama held onto Mrs. Kostaniuk's hand for a moment and smiled through tears that were running unashamedly down her face. Then she turned to me and enfolded me in an embrace.

"Rebecca, you'll forgive us, yes? Please say you will."

"Of course, Mama," I heard myself whisper.

"Good. We'll see you on Rosh Hashanah then. Don't worry. Soon it will all be better." Gently she placed her hands on my shoulders, then stepped away from me, turned, and walked slowly out the door.

I stood there for what seemed to me to be the longest moment of my life. The door swung shut behind Mama. Mrs. Kostaniuk paused and then bustled over to me. I was ushered into the kitchen and given an apron. I put it on without question, too stunned to really follow what was happening.

But in no time Mrs. Kostaniuk had me rolling dough for perogies, and was teaching me how to fold them and stuff them with a filling of potato and a little cheese. Mrs. Kostaniuk chattered away, and although I only understood about one word out of ten, the warmth of the stove, the work, and her good cheer eventually had a salutary effect. By the time I heard the outer door open I was even able to manage a small smile for Mrs. Kostaniuk. Maybe, I thought, I'll survive this after all. It was a nice clean home, just as Zaida had said. And they had lots of food. My stomach was rumbling. I realized that I was famished — I'd hardly eaten properly at all since the fire. And if it were only for a little while, well, I could stand that. And I'd see the boys at school the next day.

A girl hurried into the room. If there could be an exact opposite of me, this girl was it. Where I was tall, she was short; where I had long dark hair, hers was blond and cut at the shoulders; where I was thin, she was round, just like her mother. She had a face covered with freckles, a small turned-up nose and blue eyes. She reminded me of the pictures of Dorothy in my Oz books — she even wore a big yellow ribbon in her hair, just the way Dorothy always did. Mrs. Kostaniuk said her name, Sophie, and then pointed to me and said my name. So this was to be my new friend — according to her mother, at least.

I held my breath, wondering how she would feel about my being there. She walked over to me, took my hand and shook it, pumping it up and down until I feared she might break some bones. Her hand was half the size of mine but strong — maybe from rolling all those perogies. I giggled to myself. Sophie noticed my smile and hers grew even broader. She spoke quickly to her mother in Ukrainian, then, in excellent English, asked me if I had seen my room yet. I shook my head.

"I suppose Mama has had you in here cooking all afternoon," she said. She didn't wait for my reply. "Come with me." She led me up a narrow flight of stairs. There were three bedrooms on the second floor. Sophie motioned for me to follow her.

"You and I will share a room. The boys share the others. My parents sleep in a room off the living area downstairs."

There were four doors. Proudly Sophie opened the fourth door to reveal a wooden toilet seat and a sink and a round washtub. "An indoor bathroom!" she exclaimed. "Papa put it all in last year. It's what he does for a living. It's the rage."

I was deeply impressed. Why, they must be rich! A father who installed indoor toilets! I tried not to think about my papa who seemed incapable of doing anything at all.

"And the bathtub," Sophie bragged. "Look at it! We can fill it halfway up with water and wash everything at once, even our hair!"

I let out a sigh of wonder. This was true luxury!

"You do speak English, don't you?" Sophie said, hands on hips.

I blushed. "Of course I do," I replied. But the truth was I was overcome with feelings of shyness and her outgoing manner just made me feel that whatever I said would sound silly.

"Ah, good, I thought for a minute they'd landed me with someone who never learned." She grinned. "That was a joke." When I didn't respond she said quickly, "I'll bring up your bag, and help you unpack." Before I could tell her that she didn't need to, that I would do it myself, Sophie was down the stairs and back up, suitcase in hand. I had very little. The clothes I was wearing were the clothes I'd worn the night of the fire. I'd been given some hand-medowns from the Hebrew Ladies Aid Society: a sweater, a pair of winter boots and a jacket, an extra skirt, black, one extra blouse, bright blue, two pairs of stockings, and the suitcase.

Sophie didn't say anything nasty about the wretched state of my belongings. What she did say was, "Mama told me your house burned down."

"Yes."

"That must've been terrible."

"It was."

"Did you have a favourite doll you lost?"

I stared at her, quite taken aback. How could she know that? I had mentioned it to no one, had forced myself to not even think about such an unimportant matter as a doll. After all, I was twelve! Far too old to be attached to such things. But when Sophie said it, tears sprung to my eyes.

"Miss Perfect," I answered. "That was her name."

"Like you."

I frowned. What did she mean by that? Was she already making cruel jokes at my expense?

"No, no," Sophie said, obviously seeing that she had upset me. "I mean that as a compliment. You're so pretty. And tall. And neat. Look at your braid. Not a hair out of place. Look at my hair. Always out of control."

"Me, pretty?" I exclaimed. Now I knew I was being mocked. "I'm too tall, and terribly ugly," I protested.

Sophie's eyes opened wide in disbelief. "You aren't! You're, you're, well, you're pretty and that's that! Now, what do you like to do?"

"To do?"

"Yes. For fun!"

"Oh, I like to read."

"Do you? So do I! Would you like to borrow a book? I have three out right now from the library, but I just finished one. It's called *The Prince and the Pauper,* by Mr. Mark Twain."

"But I love Mr. Twain," I exclaimed.

"You do?"

"Yes," I said, suddenly forgetting to be on my guard with her. "Not as much as Mr. Baum though."

"Mr. Frank Baum? Who wrote *Dorothy and the Wizard in Oz?*"

"Yes! Have you read it?"

"Of course! Whenever a new one comes out I read it. He's my favourite author! My favourite of his books so far is *The Land of Oz,* where Tip is enchanted by the witch."

"Oh, oh," I said, "mine is *Ozma of Oz* where Dorothy meets the Wheelers. And she finds herself in a land where lunch boxes grow on trees!"

"And Billina the chicken can talk and becomes her friend!" said Sophie. "And they meet the Nome King!"

I clapped my hands in glee. "The Nome King! He is so bad! And yet, somehow, I just can't hate him."

"Me either!"

We stopped for a minute, stared at each other, then burst out laughing. I think we each knew something at that moment, the way you know a thing is true without it being explained. We had each found a friend. A real friend. And

I had been dreading this so much. I almost hugged Sophie, I felt so relieved!

"Come," said Sophie, "we must go help Mama with the dinner." I could smell the perogies frying. "We have some carrots to peel. Mama bakes them with raisins and sugar to go with the perogies."

"My Baba makes a dish just like that," I said. And I gladly went down to help, my heart feeling as though a weight had been lifted from it.

"The boys are still working," Sophie explained. "Sasha helps in Kozynsky's furniture store after school. He'll be home after six. The other boys work until then too." I found my butterflies returning. I knew boys. If they didn't like me they could make my life miserable. In fact, if they *did* like me they could make my life miserable. Look at Max!

Shortly after six the boys came home. First Sasha came into the kitchen and Sophie introduced me to him. "This is Rebecca," she said, "who has come to stay with us for a little while." He shook my hand very politely, and gave me a little wink as if to say, "You'll be fine, don't worry." He looked very like his sister, blond with blue eyes, but he reminded me immediately of Max — something about the twinkle in his eyes. Then two more brothers walked in, who Sophie introduced as Vladimir and Piotr. They nodded curtly to me and began to wash up. They were both dark-haired with swarthy complexions. Then Sophie's father stalked silently into the kitchen without a word or a glance at anyone. He washed at the sink until the water in the basin was black, drained it, filled it and washed again. The children all said "Hello, Papa," politely. He grunted something in return. Then Sophie pointed to the table, motioning for me to sit. But I felt far too embarrassed. How could I just sit down at this table, beside all these strangers? All my fears and anxieties flooded back. I stood awkwardly, wishing I could simply disappear. How could I have been so silly as to imagine that one happy moment with Sophie would change the fact that I was in their home as a charity case?

The father sat, followed by the boys. Again Sophie pointed to a chair, but I was frozen to the spot.

Then the father spoke in Ukrainian, but I caught the word Yid. It was something about my being Jewish, I was sure of it. He looked at me as if I was a bug.

Mrs. Kostaniuk answered. It sounded as if she were lecturing him. He looked at me again and said in English, "Sit."

I sat. The father bowed his head and so did the boys who were seated. Sophie and her mother were getting ready to serve the food. The men clasped their hands in prayer. I didn't know what to do. I couldn't pray a Christian prayer! Why, Papa, a free thinker, didn't believe in prayer at all! Zaida and Baba said the blessings, but they were sure to be different than these. I was so panic stricken I thought I might faint so I stared ahead and did nothing. To my relief, the father ignored me and when the blessing was finished, the meal was served. But although I had been so hungry just moments earlier, now I couldn't swallow. The father hated me. I could see that. So why was

I there? I supposed it was the mother who had decided — so I was an unwelcome guest, at least for part of the family. Exactly what I'd dreaded.

Chapter Seven

Dinner was excruciating. I quickly realized that Mrs. Kostaniuk was urging me to eat and wouldn't be satisfied until I did so. Not eating was simply drawing more attention to myself so I forced myself to swallow. The father barely spoke a word but the others chattered away, usually in Ukrainian, sometimes slipping into English. I didn't utter a word. Every once in a while I noticed the father glaring at me. Was that because he hadn't wanted any foster child? Or was it because I was a Jewish foster child? I thought of the kitchen table back on Selkirk Avenue, of Max and Shmuel and Fanny and how desperately I wanted to be with them. And what of Leah and Solomon? Were they as unhappy as I was? Maybe it wasn't as bad for them. They were younger. They'd get used to it faster. Or maybe it was worse because they couldn't really understand what was happening. At least, Leah couldn't. I felt the tears stinging my eyes again.

Sophie noticed and nudged me. "Let's clear up," she

said quietly. I was glad to do it, relieved to be away from the father's glare. After dinner Sophie led me to her room and she handed me the promised book. She didn't try to talk to me or make any jokes, as if she knew I was too frail at that moment to pretend everything was all right.

We had one lamp to share on a table between the two beds. We lay on our stomachs and moved as close to the lamp as we could and I began to read. In no time I was so deep into Mark Twain's story of two look-alike boys that I forgot about everything. There was a small bureau in the room and Sophie sat down there to do homework at one point. Soon it was time for bed.

I felt a little better by the time we went to sleep. I had been reminded by my reading that everyone met with adversity. How would I behave, that was the real question — by feeling sorry for myself, by being angry and bitter? Or by being brave? I had never seen myself as a brave person. Max was the brave one. But that didn't mean I couldn't try. I'd have to try.

I awoke the next morning with a jolt, strange sounds all around me, strange smells, strange surroundings. For a brief moment I had no idea where I was. Then it all came rushing back to me. I pulled the cover over my head. My resolve to be brave from the night before had completely evaporated. Now I had to face a new school. And everyone would quickly learn that I was some poor outcast. I'd be despised.

"Come, sleepy-head," Sophie chided me. "We have to help Mama with the breakfast."

I dressed and then used the family bathroom. Running

water to wash your face, and a toilet that flushed inside! It was amazing. I hurried downstairs to join Sophie and Mrs. Kostaniuk in the kitchen. Frying in a large pan were thick slices of meat — but meat I'd never seen before.

"What is that?" I whispered to Sophie.

"Bacon, of course," Sophie answered.

"Oh," I said, feeling my cheeks burn. Pork. I had never eaten *traife* food. I could, though, according to Papa. Being a free thinker, he didn't believe in the laws of *kashrut.* But Baba certainly did, so I'd never eaten pork or even seen it before. It smelled strange to me, strong and greasy.

"You can have some bread and butter and preserves," Sophie said, translating from her mother. "The boys like the meat before they work. It's such a long day."

The father walked in and this time didn't even acknowledge my presence. Why was he being so mean to me?

Everyone ate quickly, the boys shovelling back their food in minutes. Sophie and I washed up the dishes, then went upstairs to finish getting ready. I braided my hair and put on my sweater. Sophie tried to make her hair behave by putting water on her brush, but finally she exclaimed, "Oh, it's impossible!" I offered to help but Sophie's hair seemed to be like Max's — not to be tamed.

Sophie and I left for school together, Sasha having gone ahead earlier with some friends. We had to walk a number of blocks before we got to Strathcona School. I kept hoping we would run into Max and Shmuel but we didn't. Finally we arrived. It was a huge building, three stories high! I thought back to our tiny little schoolhouse in Oxbow and wished a cyclone could pick me up and drop me there, like Dorothy's twister dropped her in Oz. The schoolyard was filled with hundreds of children all playing on the brown grass. Still, grass was better than the dry mud that I had noticed was everywhere in Winnipeg. As we walked through the crowds of children I heard a myriad of different languages — Yiddish, Russian, German, English, Ukrainian, Polish.

Suddenly Sophie put her hand on my arm. "Oh no," she said, her voice low.

"What?" I asked.

"Over there — it's Sasha. He and his friends — they're always fighting! I try to tell Mama but she won't listen. She says boys fight and that's that. Honestly!"

I smiled. "Max is like that," I said. "He's like my brother, although actually he's my uncle. He loves to . . . "

I stopped in mid-sentence. I took a step closer. A crowd was beginning to gather around the boys who were fighting — and I quickly saw that it was Sasha and Max! Then about six other boys joined in, all against Max. Over the cries of the schoolyard I could hear the words, "dirty Jew." I felt the blood freeze in my veins. I hadn't heard those words since I'd been a child in Russia. I looked at Sophie to see her reaction. Sophie's face was bright red and she was shaking her head. "I'm sorry, Rebecca," she said. "He doesn't really mean it. He just likes to pick fights."

I didn't bother to answer. I tried to break through the crowd. I wasn't going to let Max get hurt — I'd fight too if I had to. But before I could get too near them Shmuel joined Max, as did another group of boys — I thought perhaps they were Jewish, because they fought Sasha's gang with a frenzy.

The school bell rang. Sasha called to his group, "Come on, not worth getting in trouble for these Yids. Let's go." They turned and headed for the school.

"Max! Shmuel!" I ran over to them. The other boys in the group began to squeal, "Max! Shmuel, you're my hero! *Ooooh.*"

Max grinned. He muttered something to them, probably about our being related. They hurried toward the school entrance. Max and Shmuel walked with me.

"Nice way to start our first morning," Max said, trying to catch his breath. "But I think we taught that miserable excuse for a human a lesson."

"That miserable excuse, as you call him, lives in the house I've been sent to," I told him.

"What?"

"He seemed perfectly friendly to me," I said. "I don't understand. His sister seems truly nice . . . mind you, his father looks at me as if I'm some kind of worm."

"Papa said they're very religious," Shmuel said, reaching down to brush the dirt off his pants. "The mother feels it's her duty to take in those in need."

"The mother, maybe," I commented. "The father seems very unhappy that I'm there and he said something in Ukrainian about a Yid . . . "

"Obviously the son feels the same," Max snorted.

"Did you hear what he called us?" Shmuel said.

"Yes."

"They're going to learn very quickly that they can't push us around or scare us. Probably a surprise to all of them," Max said. "At recess you and Shmuel come find me. Stay away from those Ukrainians if you can — including the sister."

Outside the school the children had formed into lines, the girls forming a double line in front of one door, the boys in front of the other. Max, Shmuel and I hung back until all the rest were inside and then we entered together. I followed the two boys to the school office. There a young woman with swept-back blonde hair and red lip rouge wrote our names down. She marked down our ages, asked each of us to tell her in English what our favourite subject was and asked us each questions about the farm, explaining that she wanted to get an idea about how proficient we were in English. She then wrote our class numbers on a piece of paper. It wasn't until we were in the hallway that Max read the room numbers aloud and I realized that we were all in different rooms. Things just kept getting worse and worse.

My heart thudded as I walked, all alone, down the now silent hall, looking for my room. My class turned out to be on the second floor. I reached the room and stood there for what felt like hours trying to work up the courage to enter. Finally I knocked on the door. A young woman answered. She had reddish-blond hair, green eyes, and a smile that covered her entire face. "A new student?" she asked.

I nodded.

"Please come in."

The students were sitting at desks but they weren't working with pencil and paper in an orderly way, like at my old school. There was newspaper laid out over all the desks and the children were shaping lumps of clay.

"Please tell us your name."

"Rebecca Bernstein."

"And mine is Miss MacFarland. Well, Rebecca, have a seat at that desk with Rachel Levy. I'll get you your own piece of clay. What grade were you in before coming here, Rebecca?"

"I just started grade seven," I replied quietly.

"Well, Rebecca, we have students of all ages and abilities here. Some are advanced in math, for instance, but their English is not as good. Not all of the class speaks English fluently, so we do a lot of activities where children can work and learn and talk at the same time."

I went over to the window aisle where Rachel was sitting at a desk. I was grateful that the new teacher was so pleasant and that she'd immediately placed me with someone Jewish. I looked quickly around the room. There were many different ages — some boys looked like they might be as old as sixteen. And there were many more boys than there were girls, I suppose because most girls were probably already working full time. Something, I thought bitterly, I wished I could be doing. Then I could at least be with my own family.

I noticed Sophie sitting with a red-headed girl. She smiled at me, but I couldn't bring myself to smile back. How on earth was I going to be able to continue living at that house?

Chapter Eight

"Hello." I spoke to Rachel in Yiddish as I sat down. I was so relieved to be back with one of my own kind, I forgot all about being shy for the moment.

"Hello to you," Rachel replied, also in Yiddish. She was a rather plain looking girl with brown eyes, brown hair that looked none too clean and spots on her face. As soon as I sat down Rachel began to question me, talking low, never actually looking at me, focussing only on the blob of clay she seemed to be transforming into — a blob of clay.

"Where are you from?" was the first question.

"Saskatchewan," I replied.

"Before that?"

"Just outside of Odessa, in Russia."

"We lived in Odessa," Rachel informed me. "My father had a beautiful store filled with watches and clocks. Only the best. What does your father do?"

I tried not to squirm. "We all farmed, you see," I explained, "so he was a farmer."

"And now?"

"He's looking."

Rachel shot me a glance that could only mean one thing: You mean he's a bum.

"We just got here," I said. "He'll find something soon."

"My father got a job fixing watches as soon as he arrived here. We have a nice home already. What about you?"

I was beginning to dislike Rachel. Why was she prying? And yet I felt forced to answer. I instinctively knew that Rachel would not stand for it if I didn't.

"I'm, I'm, staying with a family, another family until my papa finds work," I said in a small voice.

"Aaah," said Rachel, "I know about you. You're the one staying with the Ukrainians. Mama heard all about it in the market the other day."

I was so embarrassed I couldn't reply. Instead I tried to concentrate on the lump of clay Miss MacFarland had put down in front of me. So everyone knew of my family's humiliation. It was just as I'd feared — I'd be the laughingstock of the school. Or, as it seemed with Rachel, the subject of pity, perhaps even contempt. My cheeks burning, I silently began to mould the clay into a face.

"Never mind," Rachel stated, "you have nothing to worry about. You're with me now and what I say goes around here. No one will make fun of you or they'll answer for it. You'll be part of our group. And you'll stay away from that family — they'll feed you and put a roof over your head but that doesn't mean you have to have anything to do with them."

I nodded mutely, feeling a mixture of relief and resentment. On the one hand, now I'd be part of a group, a Jewish group. It appeared from what Rachel had just said that she was the unofficial leader. On the other hand, who was Rachel to decide who I could be friends with?

"All right, children," said Miss MacFarland, "time to put away your clay."

Everyone got up and put the clay on the table along the back wall. "Now please pull out your readers. We'll read aloud until recess. Who wants to start?" She looked at me but I shook my head and held my breath. I wouldn't get up in front of the class and read. I couldn't! Miss MacFarland turned to a boy sitting beside me. "William, you will read please."

William was obviously from a British home — he spoke with a funny English accent. But he read well and I began to enjoy reading along and listening to the story. It was a Canadian story about a girl called Anne who was an orphan sent to live and work with strangers. Although I wasn't an orphan, the feelings that Anne had of not belonging were so close to my own that I almost began to cry, right there in school.

Fortunately before that happened a bell was rung up and down the hall signifying a recess break. Rachel nodded imperiously at me. Meekly I got up and followed her out. I noticed Sophie being pulled away by her friends. And I couldn't help feeling bad — I'd been so sure the night before that we would be good friends.

Out in the schoolyard Rachel introduced me to the

group I was now to be part of — Deborah, Lotty, Clara and Jenny.

"Now, girls," Rachel said, "it is not Rebecca's fault that her father is out of work and she is living with the Ukrainians. She's going to be part of our group and that's that. And," she added, "I want no one making fun of her!"

With an introduction like that all my shyness returned and even though the girls tried to ask me questions and include me I couldn't speak. I grunted yes and no answers and tried to become invisible. I looked desperately around for Max and Shmuel but couldn't see them anywhere.

The rest of the day passed in a swirl of misery. I didn't see the boys, even at lunch, which I had to accept from Sophie although I couldn't sit with her. I couldn't explain why, so I simply thanked her and then went to join Rachel. I couldn't help but notice the hurt look on Sophie's face. To make matters worse, Miss MacFarland announced that our class would be acting out a play that we would write ourselves. I pictured myself getting up on stage again and forgetting all my lines like last time. Only this time it would be in front of the entire school. No, I'd rather die. Even nice Miss MacFarland couldn't make me do it.

At the end of the day I rushed out, looking for Max and Shmuel. I spotted them, but they were in a sea of other faces — they were quickly forming their own gang. I felt a tentative tap on my shoulder. I turned to see Sophie, who was staring at the ground.

"If you need to walk home with me . . . perhaps you'll get lost otherwise . . . it's up to you, of course."

I nodded. I really wasn't sure of the way yet. Silently I fell into step beside Sophie. We walked to the house without speaking a word. When we got there Mrs. Kostaniuk was her cheerful self, delighted to see both of us, and as soon as we walked in the door we were put to work doing chores in the kitchen, helping to get dinner ready.

I was in the middle of peeling potatoes when Sophie turned to me and said, "Mama wants to know why you seem so sad."

I looked at Sophie. "Why don't you tell her," I said.

"I don't want to make trouble," Sophie replied, voice low.

"You don't want to tell her your brother hates Jews?" I asked. "Surely she knows that."

"No, she doesn't," Sophie objected. "Mama is deeply religious. She believes that we should love our neighbours as ourselves. Otherwise she wouldn't have offered to have you here. She knew you were Jewish."

"What about your father?" I asked. I wasn't sure where I was getting the courage to speak this way to Sophie — except that somehow I felt I could say anything to her, even things that weren't very nice.

"My father, well, my father is very religious too. More religious than Mama. I mean, going to church religious, following every word the priest says. And well, the priest never says very nice things about the Jews."

"Is that where your brother gets it?"

"I suppose," Sophie said reluctantly. "But I don't think he really believes it. Honestly, he was just looking for an excuse for a fight. I'm sure of it. He knew it'd make them mad. He wanted to show them who the boss of the schoolyard was."

I smiled a little. "He found out, didn't he?"

Sophie actually giggled. "Yes! Your cousins!"

I couldn't seem to stay mad at Sophie. I just liked her — plain and simple.

It didn't seem quite so simple when Sasha came home. He behaved as if nothing had happened. He was perfectly nice to me, asking how my first day of school was. I glared at him and answered, "Fine." But he didn't even notice I was angry. "Good," he replied cheerily, as he sat down at the table to be served. Mr. Kostaniuk walked in as he had the night before and ignored me the way he had the night before. Dinner was a terrible trial, the more so because I kept picturing the happy chaos of the Churchill kitchen.

After dinner Sophie and I went to her room to do homework. Sophie offered to help me with the Math because it turned out I was behind the rest of the class in that subject, although I was ahead in reading. We worked diligently for an hour. Then we rewarded ourselves by reading our books. I was so exhausted by the day's events that I was ready for bed very early. I fell fast asleep as soon as my head hit the pillow, which was just as well because had I lain awake I would not have been able to figure anything out. My life was too confusing. I couldn't make sense of anything, anything at all.

Chapter Nine

The next day at school Max found me in the schoolyard. "Meet me right after school," he said. I knew immediately that he was up to something.

"Max, what are you . . . ?"

He didn't let me finish. "Just meet me. Tell Sophie you won't be home for dinner."

"Can I?"

"Of course. You aren't a prisoner."

"But surely I have to ask her mother's permission?"

"Then run home at lunch," Max ordered.

When I told Sophie, she offered to go home with me over the lunch hour so she could interpret for me to her mother. We talked a little about the play and school, but it was still awkward between us. Mrs. Kostaniuk was happy to give me permission to go out with my cousins. But when I sat down at my seat beside Rachel when school started after lunch, Rachel glared at me.

"Why did you leave school at lunch to go with

Sophie?" she demanded.

I explained, but Rachel was still not pleased. "Listen," Rachel said, "it's very simple. You are part of our group. You don't spend any time with Sophie. Is that clear?"

I wanted to tell her no, it wasn't clear. Why couldn't I be friends with Sophie? But Rachel had made it quite obvious that if I dared cross her I'd be tossed out of the group and that was unthinkable. At least I belonged somewhere now, and had a gang that would protect me and include me. Sophie had her own friends at school and they obviously didn't want me any more than Rachel wanted Sophie. So I nodded mutely, and sat down with Rachel as we worked on learning how to knit.

After school I met Max and Shmuel on the playground. As usual Max looked like he'd been rolling in dirt. His hair was tousled, his face was dirty, his trousers had grass stains on them.

"What have you been doing?" I exclaimed. "It looks like you've been working on the farm, not going to school."

"This time it was the Poles who wanted a piece of us," Max replied. "They've now discovered the Jews aren't pansies to be stepped on."

"Did you fight too?" I asked Shmuel.

"Of course," Shmuel answered.

"And yet," I remarked, "you look perfectly neat, as always."

Shmuel grinned. "It is an art."

"Come on," Max said, pulling on my sleeve, "we have to hurry. We have a long walk."

"Where are we going?" I asked as we walked. Not that I

really cared. I was simply happy to be with the boys again. "And won't your papa be mad that you aren't at the store?"

"No, we asked permission," Max said.

"You asked *permission*?" I couldn't believe my ears. This was not like Max.

"Yes, we did," Max confirmed. "Of course, Papa thinks we are staying after school at the request of our teacher to get caught up on our schoolwork."

"Max!" I cried, giving him a little hit on the arm. "You are such a *gonif*!"

"You have to be a little tricky with your parents," Max replied innocently, "or you'd never have any fun."

"So where are we going?" I asked again, my curiosity now rising.

"You'll see," Max answered mysteriously. We walked toward Main Street and talked quickly, trying to get caught up on all the news.

"Shmuel and I are selling newspapers at five in the morning," Max told me. "So we've already made a little money. Of course Shmuel fell asleep in class this morning, so I'm not sure that he should continue," Max added.

"If you can do it, so can I," Shmuel insisted.

"I'm stronger than you are," Max stated.

Shmuel couldn't argue about that. It was true.

"Max is right," I agreed. "If it's going to affect your schoolwork you shouldn't do it, Shmuel. Max can do it and treat us to everything!"

"A *gonif* like me?" Max inquired. "*Gonifs* never treat, do they?"

"I take it back." I grinned. "You aren't a *gonif* at all.

You're a *mensh.*"

"Flattery will get you everywhere." Max grinned back. "So, have you made friends at school? And what about Sasha? Is he giving you any trouble at your new house? Because if he is, I'll take care of him again!"

"No," I answered, "he isn't. In fact, he's perfectly friendly. Sophie claims that he doesn't hate Jews so much as he loves a good fight and he just wanted to get you going, see what you're made of."

"Well, I think we showed him that!" Max said.

"I've been included in a group of Jewish girls," I told them.

"Good," Max said, simply assuming it *was* good.

"We've met some nice fellows," Shmuel remarked. "And once we beat up Sasha and his group we were accepted immediately. In fact, everyone wants to be friends with us."

"So Sasha did you a favour," I said, smiling.

"I wouldn't put it quite like that," Max said. Then he paused. "Look, Rebecca. We're almost there."

Ahead I saw tents, which had been erected in a large open space.

"Come on," Max urged. "I got a huge tip from a swell yesterday morning when I sold him a paper," he told me as we ran, "and I'm spending it all today!"

When we reached Matheson Avenue we stopped and stared. Above us was a huge sign: "Buffalo Bill's Wild West Show!" and "Pawnee Bill's Far East Show." I had heard of the shows, of course — who hadn't! — but I'd never dreamed I would actually see them! Max paid 60 cents each for us to get in and we stood for a moment looking around. Then we went and got seats near the back, because reserved seats were one dollar each.

The seats were placed on the grass, a large canopy covering the entire area in case of rain. Quickly the seats filled up with adults and children of all ages. Everyone was eating treats of some kind bought at the many stands set up, but Max had no extra money.

"Max," I said, "shouldn't this money go for food or some such — the family is struggling . . . " I wished it was enough to have kept me at home, but even though I knew it wasn't, I still felt guilty about our spending it on something this extravagant.

Max replied, his voice almost stern, "Rebecca, food for the spirit is as important as food for the belly."

I almost laughed, but when I looked at him closely it didn't seem he was joking. And certainly it did *my* spirit good to be anywhere with him and Shmuel again. And I had to admit I was thrilled. This was an event we could only have dreamed of in Oxbow — perhaps there *were* some advantages to the big city after all. I promised myself I would write down every detail in a letter to Masha, so she could feel a little as if she'd been here with us.

I gasped as the first spectacle began to unfold before us. Elephants — real, live elephants — lumbered onto the huge performance area, with glamorous women sitting on their backs swaying back and forth. The women wore glittering headdresses, all silver and gold, and shimmering ruby red gowns.

Walking between them were men whose bare chests

gleamed with oil, wearing tight-fitting britches made of purple suede. Their ears were adorned with gold hoop earrings, and gold pendants hung on their chests. Women, wearing pantaloons of silver and delicate lace tops, walked between the elephants as well. I was mesmerized, feeling almost as if I had entered a magic land, perhaps the way Dorothy felt when she first woke up in Oz. When the parade was over, a train, a small train to be sure, but a train, running on a track, began to slowly chug across the area. Bandits on horses attacked. Police on the train shot it out with the bandits, and a fierce battle ensued, the bandits losing in the end. The crowd roared with pleasure as the bandits were dragged off and I added my voice to theirs. I knew that it was a play, but I was relieved when the police won.

Then the Rough Riders charged onto the field on their horses, leaping off their horses, jumping back onto them, twirling their ropes, doing all kinds of fancy tricks. Steers were brought in so the riders could rope them. I held tight onto Shmuel's hand as I feared for their lives — the steers were fierce and I knew from the farm how dangerous they could be.

And just when I thought the show must be over a small group of buffalo charged across the field, followed by cowboys who staged a mock roundup. The crowd applauded and whistled and stamped their feet as the cowboys corralled the huge beasts. As the animals were removed, a woman, Miss Annie Oakley, rode her shining black mare to the centre of the field, and demonstrated her skill as a sharpshooter. A woman!

And there was more — the finale. Buffalo Bill led his troops in a battle against the Indians. The horses thundered across the field, the Indians whooped and cried their battle cry, and the Rough Riders shot their rifles, Buffalo Bill himself leading the charge.

The three of us sat there when it was finally over, not wanting to leave. What an experience! My heart was still pounding when we finally got up.

"Thank you," I said fervently to Max, as we began our walk home. "That's probably the most fun I've ever had!"

Max and Shmuel were exhilarated as well. As they walked me to the corner of Stella Avenue I thought how absolutely perfect it would have been if only we all could have gone home together. Instead I knocked on the door of Sophie's house and was quickly let in by her. She had saved me some dinner, which was very kind, and soon I found myself telling her every little detail of the adventure. She listened in rapt attention. And, I had to admit, it was lovely to have someone to share my story with — although even in my own mind I could no longer call Sophie a friend. That was against the rules. So that night I wrote it all to my one real friend, Masha, but that only made me feel lonelier. She was so far away.

Chapter Ten

Finally the first night of Rosh Hashanah arrived. When I entered the house everyone crowded around me, wanting to know how I was. What could I answer? Miserable? Living in a house where they hated Jews? I muttered that I was fine and tried not to talk about it at all.

I sat Sol and Leah down beside me on the floor. "Tell me truthfully," I said to Sol. "Are they kind to you?"

Before he could answer Leah did. "Ruth is just like you," she said. "She reads me stories and tucks me in, and makes me eat food, even if it is food I don't want to eat!"

"And Mayer is like Ben," Sol added. "He plays with me. He's teaching me how to catch a baseball!"

"And the parents?" I asked.

They both shrugged. Just like here, I thought. The parents so busy — the father working, the mother running the house — that there is little time to pay them much attention.

"It sounds as if you are in a good home," I said, and

they both nodded and then scrambled away to play with Ben, Saide and Sarah.

Papa gave me a big hug when he saw me.

"Well, Papa," I said, hardly daring to ask for fear of being disappointed, "have you found a job?"

"Soon," he said. "Soon."

Although I had tried to prepare myself for that answer, my heart sank and without a word I turned away from him, too disturbed to speak. I didn't even want to talk to him.

I searched the room for Fanny, whom I hadn't seen at all because she was going to a different school. When I found her we caught up on all the news. She was happy with her new school. She was so happy, in fact, that she whispered her new plan to me. "I'm going to go to university," she declared. She noticed my eyes widen. "I'm just as clever as Max," she said. "And if I intend to be a writer I need more of an education. I'll study English."

Well, if Fanny could, perhaps I could too, I thought. But not if Papa never found work! Then I'd be lucky to stay in school at all.

When it was time for the meal we ate chicken, *gefilte* fish and soup, and we dipped apples in honey for a sweet New Year. Everyone talked at once, the little children ran about, Uncle Morris and Aunt Shoshana announced they were expecting another baby. I was so happy to be there, I almost burst into tears a number of times. Leaving almost broke my heart.

The next morning I met the family at *shul* and visited with Max and Shmuel in the lobby. I ate dinner with my family again and didn't return to the Kostaniuks' until very late, after ten o'clock. When I arrived, Mrs. Kostaniuk motioned to me to be quiet. She put her head to one side and closed her eyes, showing me that Sophie was already asleep. I was just as glad. My throat was feeling a little sore, and I was tired.

I woke up the next morning before Sophie. As I passed her bed on my way to wash up I noticed that her face was all red. I hurried downstairs to find Mrs. Kostaniuk, and I motioned for her to follow me to Sophie's room.

Mrs. Kostaniuk felt Sophie's forehead. As she did Sophie woke up and looked at us both, wincing as she swallowed.

Mrs. Kostaniuk spoke rapidly. Sophie translated for me. "She says I'm burning," Sophie's voice was weak. "The doctor is only a few streets over. She wants you run over and fetch him."

I didn't know why one of the boys couldn't go, but I agreed. I dressed quickly. Mrs. Kostaniuk wrote the address on a piece of paper. Clutching it in my hand I ran over to the doctor's office, which was on Selkirk Avenue near Salter Street, only a few minutes away. The doctor turned out to be Jewish, a Dr. Bercovitch. Maybe Mrs. Kostaniuk thought he would come faster if approached by one of his own, I thought.

Dr. Bercovitch greeted me kindly and agreed to accompany me. He was a slim man dressed in a three-piece suit. He had a soft gentle voice. On the way I explained to him how I'd come to live at the Kostaniuks'. He nodded sympathetically.

"I'm sure your father will find a job soon," he said. "If

he likes the theatre he should look for work in one of the vaudeville houses, the Dominion or the Bijou, or he could always approach the Walker. Surely they must need carpenters and handymen and such. Your father must be handy if he worked on a farm."

I thought that was an excellent idea and wondered why Papa hadn't thought of it. Or maybe he had, but felt it would be beneath him. Maybe he thought he had to be on the stage or not be in the theatre at all.

When we reached the house the doctor examined Sophie. He spoke in English and Sophie, her voice very weak, translated to her mother.

"Madam," he said, "I am sorry to inform you that your daughter has scarlet fever. The entire house must be quarantined. No one may leave until we know how many here will catch it. I will have to inform the health authorities. You must keep her warm, give her lots to drink — chicken soup is always good — and fresh fruit like oranges. This one," he pointed to me, "will most likely get it too. If so, it might be wise to send them both to the temporary isolation hospital set up for this outbreak. Then perhaps the authorities will allow the rest of the house not to be quarantined."

I was actually starting to feel a little flushed and my throat was definitely worse. I said so to Dr. Bercovitch. He looked at my throat and declared that I too would probably have the rash by the next day. Mrs. Kostaniuk consulted with her husband, and within the hour a buggy had arrived to transfer both of us girls to the hospital. Before we knew it we were on our way.

We were driven up to a building that stood in stark relief against the blue sky on Dufferin Avenue, just in front of the Exhibition grounds. It was a rectangular wood, two-storey building that looked forlorn and a little forbidding. I didn't want to be there. I wanted to be with Mama if I were going to be ill. And they'd worry, wouldn't they, when I didn't appear at *shul* for the second day of services.

Mrs. Kostaniuk, through Sophie, assured me that she'd send Sasha to talk to the boys at synagogue to tell them where I was. Sophie and I exchanged glances. Well, that would be interesting. Sophie was slumped against the buggy seat, flushed and weak.

She spoke to her mother, then translated the answer to me. "I asked her if we couldn't stay home. But she says the men would be quarantined and they might lose their jobs. We'll be taken good care of there. Even with us gone, they might quarantine the house, but Mama will disinfect it and hope for the best."

The buggy came to a stop and we climbed out. My throat was getting sorer by the minute and I was beginning to feel lightheaded and woozy. Mrs. Kostaniuk and I had to help Sophie out of the buggy, down the walkway and in the front door of the building. Mrs. Kostaniuk gave the receptionist the note from the doctor. The receptionist nodded her head and got up from her desk. "Please follow me," she said. "Tell your mother she cannot go any further," she said to Sophie. Sophie whispered to her mother, her throat obviously hurting so badly she couldn't speak anymore. Mrs. Kostaniuk nodded and said something in Ukrainian, and backed away to the door as we were led away.

We passed some small rooms and one or two large ones, all filled with cots. It was quite noisy as children talked, laughed, cried, moaned, and sighed, and nurses in starched white uniforms moved briskly from patient to patient. We were taken to the second floor and put in a long room with about twenty other children. We seemed to be the oldest. In fact, I couldn't believe that Sophie and I even had scarlet fever. It was usually younger children, four to eight, that got it and Mama had been relieved when by the age of ten I hadn't contracted it. I knew there was a danger of it turning to rheumatic fever and damaging the heart and that's why parents feared it so much. I remember when Masha's sister had contracted it and I hadn't been allowed to see Masha for well over three weeks until Mama was sure it was safe. Now I was beginning to feel afraid, deep down inside.

Sophie and I were given cots next to each other. Sophie lay down and fell straight to sleep. I perched on the edge of my cot and looked around. The nurses could see that I was not that ill yet, so they ignored me for the moment and tended to the other children. The hours dragged by. I had nothing to do. If only I'd thought to bring a book. How sick would I get, I worried. Would I develop rheumatic fever and die? Would Sophie? I looked over at Sophie's face. It was bright red with the rash. I was terrified. Sophie could die.

I helped give some of the younger children warm drinks, but as the time passed I began to feel weak so I lay down on my cot.

"Excuse me," said one of the nurses. "Are you Rebecca Bernstein?"

"Yes."

"I have something for you."

The nurse gave me a brown package. I unwrapped it. It was *Dorothy and the Wizard in Oz.* I gasped. There was a note sticking out of it. I recognized Max's writing immediately.

Dear meshuggeneh Rebecca,

Only you could come down with scarlet fever at twelve years old! And on New Years yet. Sasha came and told us what had happened. He was actually very respectful, spoke in polite tones and seemed quite friendly. Perhaps Sophie is right and he's not as bad as he seemed at first. Your dear mama is very upset and is presently making you chicken soup, which she will send over tonight. Shmuel and I used this as an excellent excuse to skip out of services. We found a used bookstore and were able to purchase this book on a credit plan. Hurry up and get better. Sasha will send Sophie some books with his mother when she comes to visit later. They won't let us in.

Your bulvon cousin,
Max

I began to cry after reading the letter, which made my throat feel much worse. The letter made me both happy and sad. Happy, of course, that they were thinking of me, and sad, of course, to be separated from them all. Really separated.

Just when I think nothing can get worse, it does, I

thought. And that idea made me cry even harder. A nurse brought me a hot cup of tea with a slice of lemon in it and a sugar cube. "Now you drink this," she said. "It will make you feel better."

Dutifully I drank the tea, not like my zaida did by biting on the sugar cube between his front teeth and sipping the tea through the sugar, but by dropping the entire cube into the cup, watching it dissolve, then sipping it. Soon I was engrossed in *Dorothy and the Wizard in Oz*, reading about the earthquake in which the earth opened up, sending Dorothy, the driver of the buggy, Zeb, and the horse named Jim into an inner world; and about a magnificent yet dangerous city, made all from glass: a city where the Mangaboos lived.

Chapter Eleven

Around dinnertime the nurse returned with a large bowl of chicken soup. "Your mother made this for you," she said. "And there's enough for your friend." I looked at the nurse. She seemed very young herself, perhaps no more than twenty, with a clipped British accent, thin face, and lively brown eyes. She didn't smile but I liked her instinctively. "My name is Miss Watkins," she said to me.

"Mine is Rebecca. And this is my friend Sophie." Even saying the word friend out loud here in the hospital made me nervous. I glanced around, worried that perhaps someone would overhear me and report back to Rachel. I almost corrected myself, but realized it would be even worse to tell this nurse that I was a lodger, an impoverished lodger at Sophie's house.

Sophie woke up then, but was too weak to do more than take a few sips of the soup. "You won't get better that way," I said and I sat beside Sophie and fed her the soup a spoonful at a time.

Actually, I was beginning to feel awful. I was cold and my throat burned. It hurt to swallow and my neck felt swollen. And I noticed that I was starting to develop the rash too.

A little later Miss Watkins brought a bag filled with books that Mrs. Kostaniuk had dropped off. I looked through it — my Mark Twain book was there, as was the book Sophie was reading, as well as *The Wizard of Oz* and *The Land of Oz*, the first and second books in the series. Still, the overhead light was weak, there were no lamps to read by and it was getting dark, so I lay under my cover and tried not to feel so cold. Soon I was asleep.

I awoke the next morning burning up. The small child in the bed next to me was screaming and the sound pierced through me until my head felt like it was going to explode. I alternated between sweating and being racked with chills. Dr. Bercovitch came at some point and examined both me and Sophie, who kept sleeping and sleeping. I couldn't concentrate on my book; I couldn't do anything. I could barely drink the tea that the nurse kept giving me because my throat burnt too much. I drifted in and out of sleep. At some point the nurse brought me letters from Max, Shmuel, Mama, and Fanny. I managed to sit up long enough to read them.

Dear Meshuggeneh,

Aren't you better yet? Enough of this lazing around like a shnorrer. I'm sick of it already! I expect to hear you are all better by tomorrow.

Max

Dearest Rebecca,

Your papa and I are very distressed that you are ill and that you have been taken away from us at this time. I cannot bear the thought of not being able to take care of you myself, but the authorities refuse to let any of us visit you. You must promise us that you will drink the soup I send and drink tea all day long, for you have to flush this illness from you. Please force yourself since I am not there to hold your hand or put a damp cloth on your forehead. Your illness has made Papa realize how terrible it is for us all to be separated — what if Solomon or Leah should become ill and we could not be with them? He has redoubled his effort to find work. Have hope. Perhaps we will all be together again soon.

Your loving Mama
(and Papa)

Dear Rebecca,

You must hurry and get well. We have started to write a play in school and your class has been put with my class to do this project. So we will get to see each other in school every day, if you would just get well. Sasha's class has been put with Max's class and apparently they are creating some trouble. Sasha, although he was very polite yesterday, has begun to bait Max again. It almost seems like he is doing it less because he hates Jews and more because he loves to make trouble. In that sense he and Max are very similar, but I worry that one or the other of them will get carried away.

The store is doing a brisk business and the house is

beginning to feel more like a home. Of course we miss you and wish you a speedy recovery.

Your cousin,
Shmuel

Rebecca!!

You see, my little darling, you do have a flair for the dramatic! And you claim to have none! Why, who holds the spotlight now? Who are all eyes turned to? Who is the centre of attention without even being here? Why you, of course. No one can talk of anything else.

Your baba is furious with you for becoming sick. You had better stay out of her way when you get better. She is sure you neglected to wear a sweater on a cold night or did something thoughtless, which has brought about this calamity. Your zaida is very worried and asks after you six times a day. The children worry that you are in something like a jail! I, of course, am hoping you will remember every detail so one day your Fanny can make a play or short story out of your adventure. But I must insist on a happy ending! So put your mind toward getting better quickly, dearest one, I insist on it!

Your loving cousin,
Fanny

I alternated between tears and laughter as I read the letters. I forced myself to drink some of the soup that accompanied them, and some tea. Sophie also woke up long enough to drink a little. Then I drifted off once more. Still, every time I woke up I reached for the cup the nurse left by the bed and drank as much as I could. An orange appeared at some point and I forced myself to eat a few slices even though it hurt my throat terribly. Night came and I felt worse and worse. I huddled under the blanket shivering and shaking and had dreams of a fire that was burning the house but seemed to be burning me as well.

I awoke in the middle of the night to some kind of activity. It was dark and there was little light, but after a while I realized that something was wrong with Sophie. Dr. Bercovitch arrived and listened to her heart. "She must be given medicine to bring down her fever," he instructed the nurses, and handed them something. "Also, she is to be bathed in cool water every hour and she must be made to drink."

After he left I could hear Sophie moaning and muttering, even whimpering at times. I knew that Sophie was deeply religious and that she believed in God. So when all was quiet and the nurses had gone for a moment I put my feet onto the cold floor and staggered over to Sophie's bed.

"Sophie?"

Sophie opened her eyes.

"Rebecca? Is that you?"

"How are you?" I whispered.

"Not so good," Sophie whispered back.

"I'm going to pray for you," I told her. "And I'll pray to your God. "I knew that for the Jews God was God, the same one for everyone, but I didn't know if Sophie or her family believed that. "Don't worry. He'll hear me. And I'm sure your family is praying. You'll be better by morning."

I crept back into bed. I was sweating profusely. My throat was so sore I almost cried. I curled up in bed and did as I'd promised.

"God," I prayed, "please don't let Sophie die. Or me. Or these other children. That's all."

And before I knew it I had fallen asleep again.

When I woke up the next morning my throat was better, my chills and sweats were gone, and my rash was fading. I sighed with relief. I was over the worst, I could feel it. I turned my head to look at Sophie. She was sleeping peacefully. I sat up slowly in bed. Miss Watkins hurried over. "You look much better, dear," she said.

"How is my friend?" I asked.

"We think the worst is over. She had a crisis last night and just an hour or so ago her fever started to come down. Now, let's get some tea into you, and some fruit. They'll let you both go home as soon as they know your fever is gone."

"Home," I thought, suddenly discouraged again. "If only I had one."

Chapter Twelve

By early afternoon both of us were sitting up. I was suddenly hungry and ate an orange, an apple and a piece of bread with a little butter on it. I drank all the tea I was offered. Sophie also began to drink, and managed to eat a little fruit. Our cots were very close together so we were able to talk easily.

I told Sophie what life had been like on the farm, and Sophie told me what it was like to grow up the baby girl in a family of tough boys. Finally Miss Watkins had to force us both to rest our throats and have a nap. Before we did, though, Sophie took my hand and said to me, "I know you prayed for me. I remember. I don't care about Sasha and Max. I feel in my heart that you are my best friend."

Without stopping to think I answered, "I feel the same thing in my heart." And I gave her a kiss on the cheek.

I woke up to find Miss Watkins walking over to my bed with another letter. This one was from Papa.

Dearest Rebecca,

I have been very upset at the thought of you all alone in that strange place. You deserve a nice home and I am going to make sure you have one. So here is my news. I have found employment! A newspaper called "Der Kanader Yid," the Canadian Israelite, has hired me. It seems that all my self-education and reading has a practical application, after all. I am to review the theatre in Winnipeg for the newspaper, write articles on books, interview artists, etc. Unfortunately the pay is very poor. But along with your mama's job I believe we can save enough to have our own little apartment in two or three months! So you must hurry and get better!

Your loving Papa

I couldn't believe it. It turned out Papa wasn't such a *schlemiel* after all! But three months! That would feel like forever. Zaida had gotten a loan to start his business. Maybe Papa could get one to rent an apartment. I would suggest it. I would beg him to ask. And if he didn't I would ask whoever was in charge. Just the thought of having to return to Sophie's house made me want to cry. Not because of Sophie, but because of the father and his coldness to me. And because of the boys. It was horrible to be in a house where you weren't liked. Especially when all I really wanted was to be liked.

Sophie woke up and I told her the news from Papa's letter. She almost looked disappointed.

"It's wonderful for you," she said. "It's just . . . I love having you live with us. We can be best friends, I know we can, and I won't be the only girl in the house and after a while you'll be just like one of the family."

"No," I answered, able to be honest with Sophie in a way that continued to surprise me. "You know that isn't true. Your father and the boys will never accept me."

"Who cares about them!" Sophie exclaimed. "They are blockheads!"

I laughed. "That's what I always call Max." I paused. "In *The Land of Oz* the girls take over the government, remember? They say men have ruled for too long."

Sophie grinned. "I remember."

"I wonder if girls could ever rule here, in this world?" I mused.

"Why not?" Sophie demanded. "We are certainly as smart as the boys!"

"Smarter!" I interjected.

"So, we could."

"It would help if we had a couple of good witches on our side, like Ozma of Oz did," I commented. I looked at Sophie. "How do you feel?"

"So much better. My throat still hurts, but not as badly. What about you?"

"The same. Only I'm starving!"

We ate more soup for our dinner and after dinner found that we were tired again. We were both soon asleep.

* * *

"Fire! Fire! Fire!"

I knew I was dreaming. I wished, though, that the dream would go away.

"Fire! Children, wake up! Children, get out of bed! Hurry! Hurry!"

I opened my eyes. I could smell smoke, but I couldn't see any. I hoped that was a good sign. I looked at Sophie who was sitting up in bed. Sophie quickly put on her slippers. "We have to get out of here," she exclaimed.

All the young children in the room began to cry or scream. Many called for their mamas. I grabbed for my sweater and put on my slippers. Quickly I looked around.

In the bed next to me was a little girl who looked to be around five years old. I picked her up. "Let's go!" I ordered Sophie. Sophie grabbed a slightly older child from the bed across from us and pulled her by the hand. "Follow me," she said.

We hurried to the corridor and headed for the stairs.

"Use the back stairs," a nurse screamed. "The fire is coming from the front, below us."

We didn't know where the back stairs were. More children streamed out of our room. Sophie grabbed another by the hand, and I ordered one to hang onto my sweater.

"Children, stay with us," I shouted.

Miss Watkins ran over to us. "The back stairs are that way. Just follow the corridor. I'm going to find more children."

It was difficult to get there, however. The children Sophie was holding onto were too scared to move and the one hanging onto my sweater was pulling hard the other way. I knew I had to think of something to get them moving.

"Back there," I said, shifting the child I held to one arm

for a moment so I could point, "is a huge fire monster. Over there," I said, pointing, "is a good fairy." I spoke in English, then repeated it in Yiddish, and Russian, and Sophie said it in Ukrainian. The children forgot their terror for a moment, long enough to be herded down the hall.

"Come along," Sophie encouraged them, "the good fairy is waiting for us."

"Hurry!" I called, "The monster is coming. Hurry!"

The approach seemed to work. The children followed us. Finally I found the stairs. By then about ten children surrounded Sophie and me. We hurried them down the stairs and out the back door.

A shock of freezing cold air hit us and for a moment I couldn't catch my breath. Behind us screams and cries of terror echoed from the large building. I put the child I was carrying down and turned to find Sophie. Sophie was gathering all the children in a group, organizing the older children to watch over the younger ones.

I paused for just a minute before grabbing Sophie's hand. "We're the oldest in there," I yelled, to be heard over the noise. "I'm going back to get more children."

"I'm coming with you," Sophie yelled back.

Holding hands we raced back into the building, and ran up the stairs to the second floor. Nurses were carrying children to the back stairs, but they needed help. Seeing us, one of them called, "There are little ones in that room. See if they are all out!"

Sophie and I ran into a room halfway down the hall. It had a few cribs as well as cots. I picked up a child of about two years old, who was beet red from crying, or maybe the rash. Sophie picked up a child of around four. We hurried out of the room. Older children of five or six were milling about in the hallway crying, one of the nurses trying to round them all up. When she saw us she began to push the little ones after us. "That way, children. Follow those two girls." Soon we had another group outside.

"Once more?" I asked Sophie.

We could hear the bells of the fire wagons. Sophie, a grim look of determination on her face, nodded and we ran back into the building.

The smoke was thicker now. Halfway up the stairs, we could barely see and we began to cough terribly. We staggered back to the room with the youngest children. It seemed empty. We checked each bed and each crib and were about to leave when I thought I heard something. Someone whimpering. I looked everywhere but couldn't find where the sound was coming from.

"Do you hear it?" I asked Sophie, frantically.

"Look under the beds," Sophie suggested.

We did and finally I found a girl of about four hiding under one of the cots. "Come out," I coaxed. "We'll take you outside." But the girl was too frightened to move. I tried to push her out but she wiggled out of my grasp. The air was getting worse and worse. We could barely see.

"We'll have to lift the cot!" I decided.

Each of us took one end and we simply lifted the cot away from the child. I grabbed one of her hands, Sophie the other. We dragged her forcibly from the room and down the hall. We were the last ones; no one else seemed to be there. Coughing, eyes burning from the smoke, we ran down the corridor, pulled the child down the stairs, and finally were outside.

We sank down on the ground, both of us suddenly too exhausted to move. Someone wrapped us in blankets at one point and pulled us farther away from the building, which was, by then, engulfed in flames. Everywhere children were crying for their parents and nurses were comforting them and trying to keep them warm. I wanted my parents, too.

Chapter Thirteen

Everything was chaos. Children cried. It was cold. Families began to arrive on foot or in buggies; some automobiles puttered into the area, honking their horns; the fire wagon bells were still clanging. Sophie and I shared a blanket, sitting on the ground, shivering with cold, too exhausted from our efforts to think what to do next. And then, suddenly, Max was there, and just behind him, Sasha.

"Max!" I leaped up and threw my arms around him. Despite himself he hugged me back. And it was the same with Sasha and Sophie.

"How did you get here?" I asked.

"Someone knocked on our door screaming the place was on fire. You know how word travels. I've come to take you home. Papa sent me. As long as you are no longer contagious, Mama says."

"I'm not!" I exclaimed, thrilled. "I'm not! My fever is gone."

"I have the same orders," Sasha said to Sophie.

"Actually," he added, "I thought I'd have to rescue you!"

I looked at Max. "I suppose you were hoping for the same thing," I said.

"Don't be silly," Max replied. But I knew I was right.

Sasha and Max eyed each other warily. "You want to say something to me?" Max asked.

Sasha paused, obviously tempted. But looking at the pathetic state his sister was in, he shook his head and put his arm around her back. "Come on," he said, "we'll have to walk."

"I don't think I can," Sophie said in a small voice.

"She's still very weak," I protested. "She can't possibly walk that far."

But there seemed to be no alternative. If we waited for the authorities to help we would wait forever. So, supported by the boys, we gathered our strength and began to walk away from the fire.

The walk seemed to take forever. At one point it became time to separate from Sophie, but I barely had the strength to say goodbye. It took every bit of energy I had to put one foot in front of the other. A couple of blocks from home Shmuel met us.

"Max was gone so fast I couldn't find him!" Shmuel declared. "I've been looking everywhere for you two."

Between them the boys almost carried me to the little storefront on Selkirk Avenue. Tears began to trickle down my cheeks as I was taken into the kitchen. I was back with my family! My baba and zaida were awake, as were all the older children.

Fanny exclaimed, "My goodness, Rebecca, you *are*

one for the dramatic."

Baba put me in a chair, covered me in a blanket and put a steaming bowl of soup in front of me. "Eat," she ordered. I obeyed.

"How could there be a fire in such a place?" Baba railed. "Someone was careless, that is for certain!" She felt my forehead. "No fever. Good."

"You can have my bed," Fanny offered. "I'll sleep out here in the chair. Tell us what happened."

"It was awful," I sighed. "Sophie and I helped get some of the children out. I think everyone escaped."

"Well, well, a heroine we have here!" Baba said. "You had to help? You should have looked out for yourself!"

Zaida gave me a kiss on the forehead. "We were worried, little one," he said. "But who would think to worry about a fire — we were worried over your illness!"

"I'm better now, Zaida," I said, feeling the warmth of the soup heat me. "But I feel terribly tired."

"Of course you do!" Baba exclaimed. "*Oy!* In bed this instant! And the rest of you too!" Within minutes I was snuggled into Fanny's bed and quickly fell into an exhausted sleep.

I slept most of the next day, in fact. Mama came over and cried and cried. Then Papa came over and he cried too. I managed some more soup at some point, and Dr. Bercovitch came to check me, fetched by Max.

"She's on the mend," he said. "But I want her to rest for a full week before she returns to school." I smiled to myself and fell back to sleep. A full week at home. No school. No Rachel. Would I have to go back to Sophie's at the end of the week? Probably, but I refused to think about it.

My first day home Mama stayed and nursed me all day. The second day Mama went back to work. By then I was able to be on my own. Baba checked on me from the shop and otherwise it was lovely and quiet.

Neighbours began to drop by the next day and soon it became apparent that Sophie and I were being talked of as heroines. The nurses told how we'd gone back into the fire and helped, even though we were only children ourselves. Our names were in the *Winnipeg Free Press.* Max brought the paper home.

"Rebecca! Look. See. Here's your name. Miss Rebecca Bernstein! What do you think?"

I couldn't believe it. The children began to ask me to tell the story of what happened. Finally I was allowed out, but not far, so I went to Myersons' store next door. Mrs. Myerson wouldn't let me pay for my lemon drops. "You are a brave little girl," she said.

"I'm not!" I exclaimed. "I was so afraid."

She looked at me solemnly. "But that is what makes people brave. If you do something even though you are afraid. If you weren't afraid you'd be a *bulvon*!"

The days sped by. Finally the doctor said I was well enough to go back to school. Papa and Mama came over that night to talk to me.

"Papa, please let me stay here," I begged.

Mama answered. "Darling, Fanny has been sleeping on a chair for a week with no complaint. It isn't right."

"Papa, why can't you get a loan so we can move sooner?" I asked.

"They give you loans to start a business," Papa said. "Not to rent an apartment."

"But couldn't you try? You haven't even tried."

"I haven't because I could never pay it back, Rebecca," Papa explained. "If I were starting a business I would hope to make money. But I'm employed at a low pay and it won't go higher. So we must save, and look for a nice place, a small place to start. I won't have us live in one of those slums on Jarvis. We have to be patient."

"I thought you'd made friends with Sophie," Mama said. "And that Mrs. Kostaniuk is so nice."

"She is." As for the friend part, I didn't know what to say. Sophie and I were friends. But once back at school, what would happen to that friendship? I didn't try to explain. Papa and Mama didn't believe in religion or differences between people. They wouldn't understand why I might have to choose Rachel over Sophie. So I said nothing.

I was allowed to stay for Yom Kippur. We all went to the Beth Jacob *shul* where Rabbi Kahanovitch presided.

The women wept copiously up in the balcony, moved by the cantor's heart-wrenching singing of the prayers. I felt that I was starting a New Year just lucky to be alive; and, as I thought about it, lucky to have my family healthy. But if only we could be together again!

* * *

The next day I returned to school, and from there I was to go to Sophie's house.

As soon as I got to the schoolyard Rachel and the group found me.

"Well!" Rachel exclaimed. "You are a dark horse! Who would have thought you would do such a thing!"

"Tell us what went through your mind," Deborah said, "just before you ran back into the fire!"

"I think," I answered, "if I'd taken the time to let *anything* go through my mind, I'd never had done it."

"But what was it like inside?" Lotty asked. "Could you even see anything?"

"At first we could," I began to answer, but Rachel interrupted.

"Honestly, we won't hear anything properly as long as everyone is talking at once. I will ask the questions."

I hadn't noticed that everyone was talking at once. It was typical of Rachel to want to control everything, even conversations I had started with the other girls. Quickly Rachel took over the questions and just as quickly I lost my desire to talk. Perhaps that was what she wanted. She hated anyone taking the away attention from her. I was relieved to finally hear the bell sound.

Miss MacFarland welcomed Sophie and me back warmly. And the principal, Mr. Sisler, a tall man with a big black mustache, came to the room and told everyone how proud the school was to have students such as the two of us. My face must have been the same colour it was when I had the rash. Sophie's certainly was. At recess I wanted to go talk to Sophie but Rachel admonished me.

"Now Rebecca, I suppose you and Sophie went through an experience together," she sniffed. "But just remember she is not one of us. So we expect you to play with us at recess. Yes?"

I nodded yes. I was brave enough to run into a building that was on fire, but not brave enough to stand up to Rachel and risk all of the Jewish girls turning against me.

Sophie was actually on her way over to talk to me when Rachel took my hand and pointedly moved away, so that I ended up turning my back on Sophie. I dared not look over my shoulder. I didn't want to see the expression on Sophie's face.

In the afternoon Shmuel's class joined our class so we could jointly work on the play.

"Rebecca," said Miss MacFarland, "the play is meant to describe the people who settled here. We will go around the room, each contributing a memory, however small it may be."

When it was my turn I was too tongue-tied to speak. Shmuel must have seen my distress, and he jumped in to save me.

"Remember," he said, "when you and me and Max stayed late at school because we were using the school books for a project? And we begged to take the books home but we weren't allowed?" He gave me an encouraging glance.

"And there was a blizzard starting," I added, in a small voice.

"But we didn't want to stay in town, we all had chores to do at home."

"So we headed out for home," I added, "and we got lost because there was just white everywhere . . . we would have died if Zaida hadn't come out with the horses and a sleigh and found us."

"That would make a very dramatic scene," Miss MacFarland said to me, nodding in approval. "Is there someone you'd like to write it with?" she asked.

My heart skipped a beat. I looked quickly at Rachel, then at Sophie. What should I do? They were both staring at me expectantly. For what seemed like forever I didn't answer. Finally, Shmuel said, into the silence, "Since it happened to both of us, perhaps we could write it together?"

"Excellent," said Miss MacFarland.

I sighed with relief, but I couldn't look at either girl. Would they both be mad at me now?

Rachel came up to me as we walked out of school. "I know you would have chosen me," she said. "Wouldn't you?"

"Yes," I said.

"Next time then," Rachel said. "I'll walk you to your street." And like a little police escort Rachel walked me all the way to Stella Avenue. She made sure we walked along Selkirk Avenue for a bit, arm in arm, and that everyone saw us together. Finally she said, "Well, goodbye, Rebecca. I'll meet you here in the morning and we can walk to school together."

I nodded and turned to walk to Sophie's house. When I arrived, Mrs. Kostaniuk seemed happy to see me. She fussed over me and wouldn't let me or Sophie help with dinner. She sent us both upstairs to rest. Once in Sophie's room I couldn't meet Sophie's eyes. I lay down on the bed.

Finally Sophie spoke. "Why can't we be friends at school, Rebecca? Are you ashamed of me?"

I sat up. "No! Of course I'm not!"

"Well then?"

"Wouldn't your friends be mad at you if you talked to me at school?" I asked, trying to get out of it.

"Yes," Sophie said, pursing her lips.

"But you'd still do it?"

"Not one of them is a *best* friend," Sophie said quickly. "I'd mind, but it would be all right because we'd be together."

I looked at my toes. I couldn't answer. Why couldn't I feel the same as Sophie?

"Maybe," said Sophie, "we aren't best friends after all." And she lay down on her bed, turning her head away from me.

I felt dreadful. But I feared Rachel too much to say any more.

▣ Chapter Fourteen ▣

The next day at school Max found me just before the bell was rung. "Your father sent a message to the shop with a neighbour who was going that way. Here." He handed me a note.

Dearest Rebecca,

You have been through a difficult time. And you've had no fun at all over the last few weeks. So tonight you will meet me at the Queen's Theatre at seven o'clock. I am reviewing their new play, "The Jewish King Lear," and I have been given two free tickets. Should you want to bring your friend Sophie, or your cousins, Max and Shmuel, of course they may come, but they will have to pay for themselves.

Your loving father

"Have you read this?" I asked Max.

"Would I read your mail?" he asked.

"Yes."

"Well, I might have glanced at it quickly."

"Will you come?"

"Would I miss it?"

"And Shmuel?"

"Of course."

"I'll invite Sophie too," I said. Maybe, I thought, if I invite her, she won't be so mad at me. After all, we can be best friends, just not at school. Why can't she see that? I'm only being realistic and practical.

I stayed away from Sophie the rest of the day and walked home most of the way with Rachel as I had the day before. When I got to Sophie's house Sophie and I were once again told by Mrs. Kostaniuk to go and rest. When we were up in her room I asked Sophie if she would like to go with me to the play.

Sophie was very formal. "Thank you for inviting me," she said. "But I'd feel out of place. I can't understand Yiddish." And she opened her school books and began to study. I did the same. I felt awful — Sophie was obviously not in agreement about how we should behave at school. Why was she being so stubborn? Couldn't she see it was simpler this way?

By seven o'clock I was waiting outside the Queen's Theatre. It was housed in an old church that had been bought by a number of prominent Jews so Jewish people could have their own theatre. Max and Shmuel arrived soon after I did and then Papa arrived. He gave me a big hug and kissed me on both cheeks.

"You look so much better, little one," he said. We followed him into the theatre. "*The Jewish King Lear,*" he muttered. "Why can't they simply do *King Lear*? It's perfect. Does it need to be changed? Does it have to become Jewish?"

"Papa!" I exclaimed. "It sounds to me like you have decided you don't like this play even before you see it. That's hardly fair, is it?"

"Of course you're right," Papa agreed. "Now, I've promised to interview one of the actors who is here from New York. Why don't you three buy something to eat and get some good seats." He gave us each five cents. Five cents. I felt rich! On the other hand, I wondered if I shouldn't save it so it could help pay for our apartment.

Max, as usual, read my mind. "Five cents won't get you a place to live, dear little niece. But it will buy you a Purity Ice Cream bar." So we bought ice cream and soda water and found seats near the back, in the centre. The theatre was quickly filling up. There was a festive atmosphere. People talked, laughed, shouted to each other. I noticed a group of older Jewish boys who were making a huge racket. "Who are they?" I asked Max.

"They mostly hang out in the pool halls and hotels on Main Street," Max said. "They gamble, run numbers, play cards, make money by hustling new immigrants like us. Isaac and David have had a few run-ins with them. I think David might like them. Isaac doesn't."

Just then Fanny joined us.

"Fanny, I'm so glad you're here!" I exclaimed.

"You didn't think I'd miss a chance to go to the theatre, did you?" she said, sitting down beside me. "Besides, I love *King Lear*. Not as much as *Hamlet*, of course."

I hoped one day I could be half as smart as Fanny.

Papa rejoined us just before the theatre darkened. The curtain rose. A hush fell on the audience. But it was only a momentary hush. All over the theatre was the sound of peanuts in the shell being cracked and soda water bottles opening. I had long since finished my ice cream, which had been delicious, and I was sitting quietly, sipping my water. But the rest of the theatre patrons seemed more intent on eating than watching. People could be heard crunching away on apples and opening bags of sweets. Still, the actors played their parts as if all were quiet and eventually the audience became enthralled. What thankless children! Turning against their father in such a way. The play rolled on and soon there wasn't a dry eye in the theatre. Everyone was weeping. And finally at the climax of the play the audience held their breath as one — and that was when the gang of boys I had noticed earlier put their pop bottles on the slanted aisles and let them roll to the front of the stage, ruining the dramatic moment of the king's death.

Fanny was out of her seat before anyone could stop her and in a split second she was boxing the toughs around their ears. "You *no-goodniks,*" she hissed. "This is a play. The theatre. You'll have some respect or you'll never come back here again!"

The boys covered their ears and tried to fend off her blows. Of course, since she was a girl, they couldn't fight back, but it must have hurt to be smacked around like that by her. I started to giggle and couldn't stop. Everyone around us was saying "*shah*" so loud that no one could hear a word of what was happening on stage. So, finally, the actors stopped and then started again. This time it was quiet except for the wracking sobs of both the men and women watching. Thunderous applause ended the evening.

As we walked out Fanny was still fuming. The toughs had hurried away before she could have another go at them. Papa was fuming too. "This is a theatre? They say Kaddish, the Jewish prayer for the dead, in a Shakespeare play? If Shakespeare had wanted there to be a Kaddish in his play, he would've written a Kaddish in his play! *Oy vay*! "

He gave me a kiss and told me he would see me soon. And then Max and Shmuel and Fanny walked me home and they discussed the play all the way there. What a wonderful evening, I thought, as Max and Fanny argued over what the key meaning of the play was. But, as with the Wild West show, for me it was always bittersweet. Knowing I had to return to a stranger's house spoiled it more than a little for me, especially since there was now the added tension with Sophie. This was very apparent when I entered our room. Sophie was lying in bed reading and she didn't even look up at me, but pointedly turned a page and continued to read.

"Would you like to hear about the play?" I asked her.

"I'm busy," she answered curtly.

It was clear that I had hurt her feelings and I so badly wanted to change that, to be her friend, but how . . . ?

There was a school assembly the next day. Principal Sisler started off by describing all the teams that would be playing during the year and encouraging the boys to come to the school on Saturday for practices. There would be soccer, softball, lacrosse, and, as soon as the rinks were flooded, hockey. I knew that already Max and Shmuel were sneaking out of *shul* on Saturday to play soccer. Apparently the principal assured a special delegation of Orthodox parents that the boys weren't carrying, which was forbidden on Shabbat, but were only kicking the ball. The parents weren't happy, but most of the boys went anyway — either with permission or without.

A child from each class then read a poem about Canada. And finally Principal Sisler said to the assembly, "Now I would like to call two very special children to the front: Sophie Kostaniuk and Rebecca Bernstein." My breath caught in my throat. No! I couldn't go up there! But Miss MacFarland was pushing me out of my seat and practically walking me down the long aisle. Sophie went quite cheerfully. When we were both on stage a policeman walked onto the stage, too.

"These two girls have shown leadership," the policeman said, "something we encourage of all of our citizens. They have been brave, and by working together managed to save many children from the fire at the isolation hospital. So, on behalf of the Winnipeg Police Department and the City of Winnipeg, including His Honour, Mayor Evans, we would like to present them both with a token of thanks." He turned to us. "We are told that you each like to read and that you lost your library books in the fire. Here is a coupon that will let you choose any book (within reason) at the Folk Bookstore, right in this area. And these certificates can be posted into your new books, a certificate of good citizenship." And with a flourish he handed both of us the coupons and certificates. The entire student body burst into applause. I looked at Sophie. She was beaming with pleasure. I was simply paralyzed.

"Would you girls say a few words?" Principal Sisler asked.

I felt faint. Sophie stepped forward and said, "Rebecca and I would like to say, thank you very much. Probably everyone would have done the same as we did, right, Rebecca?"

"Yes," I managed to get out, but in a voice so small only those on stage heard me. "And thank you!"

With that Sophie turned and left the stage, with me right behind her. My cheeks were burning red. I was sure I could hear Max's distinctive whistle as I almost ran back to my seat. Soon after that the assembly was dismissed and it was recess time.

At recess all the girls swarmed around, congratulating me. But I really wanted to be with Sophie. Only Sophie would understand how I felt. I looked over to see that Sophie, too, was surrounded by her group.

Rachel interrupted everyone and ordered them all to stop fussing. "Honestly," she declared, "Rebecca did what anyone would have. Of course, Rebecca, dear," she said, "I'm very pleased for you. All the troubles you have, a poor foster child like you, well, you deserve something good. I have an entire library of books at home, but I think it was very thoughtful of them to give you one. Miss MacFarland's idea no doubt. Now, I've devised a new skipping game and I want everyone to listen while I explain.

All right, come along girls."

I stared at Rachel. She was mean and bossy. What was I doing? Without stopping to think further — not *letting* myself think further — I said, very politely, "No, Rachel, you go ahead without me. I need to talk to Sophie." And very slowly I began to walk across the schoolyard to reach Sophie and her friends. When I reached Sophie's group, they all fell silent.

"Sophie?" I said.

"Yes?"

"Would you like to walk with me?"

For a second Sophie didn't answer and my heart sank. Perhaps my offer of friendship was too late and Sophie wouldn't forgive me for being such a coward. But in the next second Sophie slipped her arm through mine and we turned together to walk around the schoolyard. We couldn't help but notice both groups of girls staring at us.

"I'm really sorry," I said. "I've been a complete coward. I didn't realize how much of one until today when they gave me that award. I didn't deserve it. You should take my coupon and get two books."

Sophie grinned happily. "Nonsense. Shall we go after school and choose our books?"

"Yes!" I said. "Will you forgive me for not being a good friend?"

"Of course," said Sophie. "We're best friends now, and no one can stop us."

Back in class I had to contend with the constant glares from Rachel but not for long. Soon we met with Shmuel's class and the time passed quickly as Shmuel and I worked on the play.

After school Sophie and I went together to go buy our new books. I felt positively lightheaded, as if I was floating on air. The world hadn't stopped even though Rachel was furious with me. And as Sophie and I walked from the schoolyard, Lotty, Deborah and Jenny ran over to me and told me that they would still be friends with me. How could I have been such a *shnuk*?

We ran and skipped all the way to the bookstore. Once there, however, we walked slowly past shelf after shelf of books. We found our favourite authors and looked over all their books. Finally, I chose *The Road to Oz*, which I hadn't read yet. Sophie chose a book she'd never read, *David Copperfield*.

"It's big," she explained, "so I can read it for longer."

The store contained an ice cream parlour. "Let's treat ourselves," Sophie suggested.

I shook my head reluctantly. I had no money.

"Let me treat," she begged. "That's what best friends do," she stated emphatically, before I could even object.

I swallowed my pride and agreed. We sat down at the counter and ordered two vanilla ice creams with cherry sauce, and two sodas. The young man behind the counter gave us generous portions and we chatted about anything and everything while we ate. The ice cream was simply divine. At some point Sophie glanced out the window and noticed it was almost dark. We hurried out — it was completely dark by the time we reached Sophie's house.

Dinner was on the table and the boys were eating. We

weren't in trouble, though, because Sasha had told his parents of the honour their daughter had received and Sophie's mother was so proud of her she could hardly contain herself. As we sat down even the father looked at me in a different way.

"It is good," he said to me in English, with a curt nod. I knew that from him that was high praise indeed. I solemnly nodded a thank you to him in return.

Chapter Fifteen

Sophie and I arrived at school the next morning to a terrible commotion. Another fight. I felt my heart begin to pound. Not again. "Please don't let it be Max," I muttered under my breath.

"Or Sasha," Sophie whispered. Holding hands we ran toward the circle that had formed.

"Who is it?" I asked Jenny who was already there, peering through the crowd.

"Max, of course," she replied. "And that devil Sasha. He has a knife."

"What?" I exclaimed, shoving as hard as I could to get through the crowd. When I was finally in a position to observe what was happening I saw that it was true — Sasha had pulled a blade out and was swiping at Max who was dancing around it, refusing to run. Shmuel was fighting with one of Sasha's friends and about ten other boys, half of them Jewish, the rest Ukrainian, were punching and kicking each other. I wanted to help, but knew that if I got in Max's way I could put him in more danger. I was desperate. This was more than one of Max's silly scrapes. He could be killed. Well, I wasn't going to let that happen. I turned and ran as fast as my long legs could carry me to the school and I did what was forbidden, an unwritten law of the schoolyard — never involve teachers. On the front steps I found Principal Sisler, who was coming to see what all the screaming was about.

"Sasha Kostaniuk has a knife!" I shouted. "He's going to kill Max!"

"No, he isn't," Principal Sisler said, as he strode across the schoolyard, me right behind him. By the time he reached the circle the children had seen him coming and had dispersed. The knife was nowhere to be seen, but Max was bleeding from a cut on the hand. Principal Sisler called out Sasha's name. Sasha stepped forward. The principal motioned for the two boys to follow him.

I followed, too, but was quickly ushered into class by Miss MacFarland. Rachel took her usual seat beside me and whispered in my ear, "That's the family of your best friend. Jew hater. You made quite a bad choice, didn't you?"

"No, I didn't." I whispered back. But inside, I had to wonder. Everyone was staring at Sophie and me and whispering. We were the centre of attention again, but this time not for being heroes.

"Class! Please, pay attention," ordered Miss MacFarland. "Today we are going to learn some songs and do some singing. Pay attention, please."

It was hard to pay attention though. I just wanted it to

be recess time so I could see how Max was. A knife. How *could* Sasha? And how could I live in that house any more? Finally, it was recess time and I ran into the playground looking for Max. He was there standing with the same group of boys. When he saw me he walked away from them for a moment so he could talk to me.

"Are you all right?"

"No thanks to you!" Max said, furious.

"What?"

"Why did you run for the principal like that? You got me in a lot of trouble!"

"But . . . but . . . he had a knife. He could have killed you!"

"He's not good enough with it to hurt me," Max scoffed.

I stared at his hand, now bandaged.

"My point exactly," said Max, "he didn't really hurt me. No, what did hurt was *this*!" Max held out the palm of his other hand. It was bright red and welts were beginning to form on the skin.

"I don't understand," I said.

Shmuel joined us then. "He got the strap for fighting," Shmuel explained. "Two lashes."

"But Sasha was the one with the knife," I protested. "Why strap *you*?"

"Oh," said Max, looking a little more cheerful, "he got four lashes and he had the knife taken away."

"The big question is what story we're going to tell Mama," Shmuel said. "She'll see your bandaged hand and if she hears you had a knife pulled on you — well, she could march over to the Kostaniuks' and spank Sasha herself. We need to think of another reason for you to have that cut." He thought for a moment. "What about a knife slipping while you were modelling the clay?"

"We'll try it," Max agreed. "And remember," he said, turning to me, "I can take care of myself." He paused. "Are you sure the sister, Sophie, isn't like her brother?"

"No!" I declared. "Of course she's not. How could I be friends with her if she were?"

"I just wanted to be certain that she hadn't bullied you into being her friend," Max said.

"Sophie's not like that at all. Really." That would be Rachel, I thought to myself. I turned back to see Sophie waiting for me. Now even Max didn't want me to be friends with her. I could tell he didn't, even though he hadn't come right out and said it.

"Don't mind him," Shmuel said to me. "Go talk to Sophie, it's all right."

Slowly I walked across the field to where Sophie was waiting for me. I felt like everyone at school was staring, wondering why I didn't stay with Max, how I could be a friend of his enemy's sister. And surely all Sasha's friends felt the same way about me.

I thought about Oxbow, then, and my friend Masha. Our friendship had always been so simple. I desperately wished I could say the same about my friendship with Sophie.

* * *

I had just sat down to dinner with the Kostaniuks when there was a knock on the door. Piotr left to answer it. I tried to avoid looking at Sasha. I was furious with him and didn't feel that four strokes of the strap was a severe enough punishment. And I was even feeling a little angry with Sophie. Shouldn't she say something to her mother? Did she want her brother to hurt someone?

A moment later Zaida was standing in the doorway of the kitchen. I was dumbfounded, seeing him standing there. I didn't know what to think. Was someone sick? Had someone died?

"Rebecca," he said in Yiddish, "go pack your clothes. You're coming home with me."

"What's wrong, Zaida," I whispered. "What's happened? Is someone sick?"

"No one is sick," he answered. "You will not live here anymore, that's all."

I stared at him for a minute, too stunned at first to move. Then I got up from the table, and said, "Excuse me." I ran up the stairs. Sophie followed me.

"What did he say?" Sophie asked.

"He told me to pack," I said, reaching for my suitcase, which was under the bed. "I'm to go home!" I stopped for a minute. "What could have happened? Do you think my papa has found us a little apartment? Oh, isn't it wonderful?"

Sophie looked crestfallen. "Of course I'm happy for you," she said, "but it's very sudden, isn't it? You'd think Mama would have been warned by the authorities, like she was before you came. I mean, it's dinnertime! Why now?"

I was throwing my few possessions into the little case. "Does it matter?" I exclaimed, bursting with excitement. I looked up at Sophie. "Don't worry! We'll still be friends. We'll be together every day at school and you can come to my house to visit and I can go to your house. It'll be just the same!" I closed the suitcase and flew down the stairs. When I reached the kitchen, however, I found Zaida in a conversation with Mr. Kostaniuk, Zaida using a combination of English and the broken Ukrainian he'd picked up in Oxbow.

Mr. Kostaniuk was obviously deeply displeased and Mrs. Kostaniuk was crying. Sasha was on his feet, his cheeks flushed bright red. He glared at me and said in English, "Someone told about the fight."

"I didn't!" I protested. "And I know it wasn't Max or Shmuel."

"It's the neighbourhood," Zaida said to Sasha in English. "A child tells a parent, a parent comes to shop to buy meat, tells us, that's the way of it . . . no secrets in Mitzrayim." Mitzrayim was the name the Jews had given to that area where so many lived — it referred back to the Jews' time of bondage in Egypt.

It began to dawn on me what was happening. "So Papa hasn't found an apartment?" I asked Zaida.

"No."

"But there's no room for me at your house," I protested. "You said so." Since we were speaking in Yiddish the others couldn't follow.

"We'll make room. You don't live in a house where they attack my sons with knives. You thank the mother, and we go."

I turned to Mrs. Kostaniuk. I knew enough Ukrainian

now to at least say thank you. "Please tell her," I said to Sophie, "how grateful I am. She's been so good to me." Then I turned to Mr. Kostaniuk and said "Thank you," and "Goodbye." I didn't know what to say to Sasha so I said nothing. Sophie walked me to the door.

"I'll see you at school tomorrow!" I assured her and kissed her on the cheek.

"Yes, at school," Sophie said trying to put on a brave face, but there were tears in her eyes.

Zaida had already started down the street — he turned back and called to me. "Come along, Rebecca. Baba is waiting dinner for you."

He had my bag in his hand. I ran after him. It was cold out and a light rain was falling. I could tell that Zaida was upset, so I said nothing on our way home. But when we got back to the house I was almost glad that Sasha had stabbed Max, because now I was home!

And yet — it wasn't quite the same. Mama and Papa weren't there. Sol and Leah weren't there. Zaida had obviously acted on his own when he'd heard, and had just stalked over there, furious. And suddenly, I felt like a relative, not a sister. A close relative, but with the nagging feeling that I didn't have the *right* to be there anymore.

Would I ever again feel like I belonged? Feel like I had a home?

Of course, I got the usual warm welcome from Fanny and Max and Shmuel. And within minutes I was sitting at the table dipping a thick piece of bread into Baba's vegetable stew, and listening to the chatter around the table. Soon I almost forgot that initial feeling. And then Zaida said something, which made that worry seem small in comparison.

"Rebecca," he said, "I understand you have become a close friend of this girl, Sophie."

"Yes," I answered, wondering why Zaida was saying this.

"Well then, Rebecca, I must tell you, that Sophie is not a good friend for you to have."

I swallowed hard. Everyone at the table fell silent. "Why?" I asked in a small voice.

"Her brother attacked our Max with a knife. The father, we hear, is an anti-Semite. You show no respect to your cousin Max by being friends with the family of his enemy. Your baba is very definite about this."

I hadn't stopped to think how angry this would make Baba — and when Baba got angry everyone knew there was no convincing her or talking to her — even Zaida was helpless in the face of her wrath.

"But . . . " I began to say.

"This is the end of the discussion," Baba stated. "So long as you are in this house, Rebecca, that girl will not be welcome. She should not be your friend."

I looked at Max for help, expecting him to stick up for me, to tell them Sophie was different, to say it was only the brother. But he said nothing, only stared at his plate. I looked desperately around the table for support, but Fanny and Shmuel were silent as well, as were the older boys and Aunt Rose. Obviously, in this case, everyone agreed with Baba.

How could I simply stop being Sophie's friend? And yet it was clear I couldn't disobey Baba and Zaida.

"What does Papa say?" I asked. "Or Mama?"

"You live here for now, Rebecca," Baba said. "Your Papa and Mama don't say anything. We've sent them a message, maybe they'll come tomorrow to see you. But it won't change my decision. Now everyone finish dinner. There's homework to do and chores left over from the shop."

I fought back tears and sat quietly at my place. I had been so terrified to become friends with Sophie. Finally, although it had taken all the courage I had, I had done it. And now . . . what would I say to Sophie when I next saw her?

Chapter Sixteen

I walked to school the next morning with Max and Shmuel. For a long time no one spoke. Finally Max said, "Listen Rebecca, I know you must be upset, but in this case I think Mama is right. It's not a nice family. Sophie would probably turn out to be a not very good friend." I opened my mouth to protest, but Max cut me off. "And even if that's not true how do you think it will look at school if you continue with your friendship? Everyone will think you have no respect for me or for Shmuel. After all, it was her brother who pulled a knife on me. Her brother who called us dirty Jews."

When he put it like that it was hard to argue. I didn't want the other children at school to think that I approved of Sasha's horrible name-calling or that I even tolerated it. And I could see Max's point, that by walking the schoolyard arm in arm with Sophie, it could well appear that I had no respect for my cousins or my Jewishness.

"What will I say to her?" I asked.

"Maybe it's best not to try and explain," Shmuel said gently. "She'll quickly understand."

At that moment I wished we would never reach the schoolyard. I knew I had to listen to my baba, and now that Max and Shmuel agreed what choice did I have? Sophie was a friend after all, not family, not close to me the way Max and Shmuel were. I couldn't go against them. And yet, why did they have to feel that way? It wasn't fair. This would hurt Sophie terribly.

I walked into the schoolyard between the two boys. Sasha stood with his gang in a corner of the yard and they immediately began to call names at the top of their lungs. Max's new friends quickly closed around him and Shmuel. I lined up with the girls.

I didn't see Sophie until I reached the classroom. She was already seated at her desk. I gave her a quick look, shook my head, and sat down. Sophie looked puzzled. I glanced over at Rachel who was watching me closely, but said nothing. When it was recess I walked out quickly with Deborah and Jenny, without a look at Sophie. My heart was thudding and I broke out into a cold sweat. It felt more like I was committing some kind of crime than going outside to play.

Rachel stood, hands on hips, waiting on the field. Slowly I walked over to her.

"*Nu?*" Rachel said.

"Can I skip with you?" I said quietly, the words almost choking me.

"Of course you can," Rachel replied briskly. The triumph in her voice was unmistakable. She was the boss of everyone once again. "Girls, Rebecca is part of our group. Yes?"

"Yes, yes," everyone agreed. They all seemed happy enough to have me back, although I noticed that Jenny, Lotty and Deborah, who had stuck by me before, almost appeared a little disappointed that I had given in to Rachel. Clara stuck close to Rachel, as I'd noticed she always did, and said nothing.

"I knew you'd come to your senses," Rachel said, "once your family talked to you. Once they knew what was happening."

Suddenly I knew how my zaida had found out about the knife. Rachel. I might have known it would be Rachel who'd cause me this trouble. "Was it your mother who told my baba?" I asked, feeling the rage build inside me.

"No offense," Rachel replied, "but my mother would never shop *traife.* She wouldn't go into your grandparents' store. But she might have said something to someone who did shop there. It's all anyone was talking about!"

I doubted that. But probably it was all Rachel was talking about, and Rachel made sure her mother would talk about it, too.

I purposefully didn't look around the schoolyard for Sophie, but Jenny whispered to me, "Don't worry. Sophie is with her Ukrainian friends. She'll be fine." I nodded and tried to hold back the tears stinging my eyes. I would not give Rachel the satisfaction of seeing me cry.

The rest of the day was a nightmare. I couldn't look at Sophie for fear that I would forget my resolve, run over, try to explain, and only make everything worse. I had to be civil to Rachel and all I wanted to do was kill her. When school was over I walked home with Max and Shmuel. I was so depressed I barely spoke a word the entire way. But much to my relief, when I walked in the door, Papa was waiting for me.

"Papa!"

"Rebecca." He gave me a big hug.

"Papa, I need to talk to you."

"I know. So I'm going to take you to Fishman's for a soda. We'll sit and talk."

My hand in his, we walked down Selkirk Avenue, stopping occasionally to talk, or to receive *mazel tov* for my bravery in the fire. We reached the little store where Papa ordered tea for himself, a flavoured soda for me, and blintzes with sour cream for us both.

"Papa, can we afford this?" I whispered.

"Rebecca, let me worry about that."

I wished he *would* worry about it. And it was even more important now.

"Papa, we must have our own home," I pleaded. "Baba won't let me be friends with Sophie!"

"And you," Papa said, "how do you feel about that?"

"Awful! Papa, we were best friends. And it took us a long time because the Jewish girls didn't want me to be friends with Sophie in the first place. And I was afraid to go against them. But finally I did — and now — now it's all ruined." This time the tears couldn't be held back and I began to cry.

"It's just like *Romeo and Juliet*!" Papa exclaimed.

"What?"

"Shakespeare's play, *Romeo and Juliet.* We are going to go straight to the library after our snack and take it out. You will read it tonight. You'll see, Rebecca, it's exactly the same story. Why, even the knife attack is similar, although the play, being a tragedy, lots of people die, and happily that hasn't happened here."

"But isn't that the story of two young people in love, Papa?" I asked, confused.

"Yes, yes, but so what? Boy-girl, girl-girl, it's about how two people love each other but their families hate each other. Just like these gangs hate each other. Why do the Ukrainians hate us? Well, in this country, most don't anymore! But in the Old Country, Rebecca, it was bad, very bad. And Sasha's father, he's still behaving like he's in the Old Country, and he's teaching all this hatred to Sasha. But you'll see when you read the play, Rebecca, it's a very old problem. For no good reason, people just decide to hate each other. And that's that. No one can convince them that they are wrong."

"But what can I do, Papa?" I asked.

"Do? Well, I'm afraid there's very little you can do. If you walk arm in arm with Sophie in the schoolyard, the other children will think you have betrayed Max and Shmuel. Now, if Max and Shmuel don't care about that, then you could do it. But I understand they do care. And your baba would still not permit it!"

"But Papa, if we had our own home, you would decide, not Baba. When will we have our own place?"

He shook his head. "I've told you, Rebecca. In a few months. It will happen, I promise. Mama has been taken on full time now. And I've been to the theatre, the Walker. They might let me work building sets. I could do that during the day, and do my reviewing at night."

I brightened. "Really, Papa?"

"Really. In fact, if the set building works out, I might do that full time so that I could act in the theatre at night. A few of us are talking of making a real Jewish theatre at the Queens, with plays by Sholom Alechim and Anski. So, you see Rebecca, maybe by January or February we'll have enough money."

"And in the meantime, you think I should not be friends with Sophie."

"On the contrary, I think you *should* be friends with Sophie. But it doesn't seem possible at the moment, does it?"

"But that's not fair!"

"And did anyone ever tell you that life is fair? I don't think so. However, you could try to convince Max and Shmuel around to your way of thinking. And then they could try to convince your baba. It seems to me that would be your only hope."

I felt a little better. Perhaps there was a *little* hope, after all. But even if I could convince everyone, would Sophie even want to be my friend anymore? Maybe, just maybe, I could defy everyone and stand by Sophie. That, however, was a very scary thought.

Chapter Seventeen

Papa and I went to the library and took out *Romeo and Juliet.* On our way home we passed Rabbi Kahanovitch who was knocking on doors, collecting money for the *shul* and for charity. He had a full black beard and wore black clothes so everyone called him the *shvartzer rebbe,* the black rabbi. I had liked the service that he'd led at Rosh Hashanah very much. My papa, being a free thinker and not believing in religion, didn't think much of rabbis in general, but even he didn't seem to mind this one. They stopped to say hello and then passed on.

Suddenly I said to Papa, "Just a minute, I'll be right back." I turned and ran after the rabbi.

"Rabbi," I said, catching up to him, "if a person wanted some advice, some advice not from a member of their own family, could that person come to you?"

"That person could find me at the *shul* just after evening prayer," he replied, "which I must hurry to, or I'll be late. That person would be more than welcome," he added.

"Thank you, Rabbi," I said.

I caught up with Papa who looked at me curiously. "Just remember what I've taught you about religion," Papa said. "It's the opiate of the masses."

"I know, Papa," I replied.

The shop was still busy when we returned. We went into the back where Fanny and Aunt Rose were cooking dinner. I began helping them. Shortly after, Mama arrived, having just got off work.

"Rebecca!" she exclaimed. "I got your baba's note. They've taken you out of that house!"

"Yes, mama," I answered.

"And, are you glad to be back?" Mama asked.

"Of course," I replied. "But Baba won't let me see Sophie anymore."

Mama gave Papa a quick, worried look. "No?"

"No. Couldn't you talk to Baba?" I asked.

"Rebecca, I can try. But I don't think she'll listen to me, do you?"

I shook my head despondently. Baba never listened to my mama.

Dinner was the usual chaotic affair and with so many people in the house it wasn't difficult for me to slip away shortly after my parents left. It was cold out, so I put on my rubber boots and a jacket I'd borrowed from Fanny. When I went out into the night it felt like it might snow. I knew I'd soon need a winter coat.

I hurried down the street to the *shul*. I peeked my head in. The men had left quite a while ago and I wondered if maybe the rabbi had gone home for his dinner too. But no, he was sitting on the *bimah*, reading a portion of Torah.

He looked up smiling. "There's always something new to discover," he said, pointing to the Torah.

"I'm sorry if I've kept you here late, Rabbi," I apologized.

"No, it's a pleasure to have a little quiet, a little time to study. A pleasure. Come, sit down." He descended from the *bimah* and sat on a bench in the front.

"You have something you'd like to discuss with a dispassionate observer, yes?"

"Yes, Rabbi, exactly."

First I introduced myself. Then I told him the history of my friendship with Sophie and of recent events and of my grandparents forbidding our friendship. When finished, I waited expectantly for an answer.

Rabbi Kahanovitch looked thoughtfully at me. "So, let me get this straight. It is not your father or mother who has forbidden this friendship, but your grandparents."

I nodded.

"But they are your father and mother for the present because you're living with them and you are under their authority; and your own parents don't wish to argue this point with them."

I nodded again.

"And what do you think my answer will be?"

I stared at my feet. "My father is not religious," I answered. "But we took Hebrew studies at school when we lived in the Hirsch colony and we read Torah. And I do remember something that was always said to us, 'Honour your father and mother.' That's part of the Ten Commandments. And since Baba and Zaida are acting like my parents, I suppose you'll tell me to obey them."

"So Rebecca, I think you suppose wrong."

"I do?"

"Your friend Sophie? Is she a good person?"

"Yes!"

"Isn't she the one who helped you save the children?"

"Yes! And she's not like her brother at all! And neither is her mother. Her mother was always really kind to me. And Sophie made me feel right at home, even though I'm shy. I can talk freely to her. We have fun. We laugh. And she's willing to be my friend even though it gets her in trouble with her gang. And," I added, "the one who makes me be her friend, the Jewish one, she's mean."

The rabbi nodded again. "There is a code of law called the *Kitzur Shulkhan Arukh*. And do you know what it says? No, of course you don't, but I will tell you. It says, as near as I can recall, 'If a father tells a child not to speak to or forgive a particular person, whom the child wants to speak to or be reconciled with, the child must disregard the command of the father.' In other words a child must listen to his or her own conscience in this regard. If a parent tells you to hate, and the person you are told to hate is a good person, well, that is wrong, isn't it? It would be different if the person, Sophie in this case, was an evil sinner. But I gather she is not."

I couldn't believe my ears. I had come to the rabbi on a desperate impulse, not really expecting any help, grasping at a straw. But he thought I was right!

"You seem a little tongue-tied, *pitseleh*," the rabbi said, calling me "little one."

"It's just, I can't believe . . . can I be friends with Sophie?"

"Now that is a trickier question. You must not turn against her. You must not hate her. But you don't want to shame your baba or zaida, do you? Or your uncles, Max and Shmuel? They must be able to hold their heads high at school."

My spirits sank. "Then I'm back where I started."

"Perhaps not. How long do you think Max and Shmuel will stay angry at this Sasha?"

"Oh, not more than a day or two." I smiled. "But Sasha will provoke them again and it will start all over."

"It seems to me that you must work on Max and Shmuel, and Sophie must work on Sasha. If you could reconcile the boys, not only would it be a step toward your reconciliation with Sophie, but it would certainly make the schoolyard a safer place! And you would have accomplished two things."

"But we could never manage that!" I protested. "Sasha hates Jews!"

"And was he cruel to you when you lived at his house?"

"Never. He was very nice to me."

"So maybe he likes to fight more than he hates Jews."

"That's what Sophie says, but I thought she was making excuses for him."

"Perhaps not. I do think you and Sophie have your work cut out. But if you can deal with the boys, then the grandparents — well, you leave them to me. But I can't help until the first thing is handled first."

"You would talk to them? To my baba and zaida?"

"I would," he said.

"My baba is very . . . " I searched for the word.

"Scary?" the rabbi asked.

I nodded solemnly. "Yes. Very scary."

"I don't scare easily." The rabbi smiled. "And somehow I don't think you do either."

"But I do!" I protested. "Everything scares me."

"Everything except burning buildings, and going against everyone in your school just to keep a friend."

I stared at him, for a moment too puzzled to speak. When he put it like that it hardly sounded like me at all. But it *was* me who had done those things. So maybe I did have more strength than I thought. And maybe I could do something about this problem.

I took a moment to think over everything the rabbi had said.

"It's funny," I remarked, "my papa said something similar to you. He said I needed to convince Max first."

"Well, there you have it," the rabbi affirmed. "We must be right. But you will have to put your brains together, you and Sophie."

I stood up. "Thank you, Rabbi," I said. "Thank you so much. I'll go to Sophie's after school tomorrow and I'll tell her what you said."

"I hope to hear good news, soon," the rabbi called, as I turned and practically ran out of the synagogue. I was so excited. There might be a way, I thought. There might be a way.

Chapter Eighteen

School passed slowly for me the next day. The lunch hour felt like it would never end. Rachel went on and on about a new suite of furniture her parents had just bought. "Oh," she said to me, "I hope this doesn't make you feel bad, Rebecca. You probably don't even have a proper bed to sleep on!" I was, in fact, sleeping on a mattress on the floor, which was definitely better than the chair.

After school Rachel insisted on walking with me all the way to Selkirk Avenue. I pretended then to be going toward the shop, but before reaching it I turned and hurried back toward Sophie's house.

Mrs. Kostaniuk was delighted to see me. "Ah, Rebecca, come, come," she said in English. She pointed upstairs to Sophie's room and motioned for me to go ahead. I raced up the stairs, paused a moment, took a deep breath for courage, then tapped on the door. Sophie opened the door. I could see that she'd been reading. Sophie was so surprised to see me that at first she didn't say anything.

Then she motioned for me to come in. Her expression was serious and a little wary.

"Sophie, I haven't been *allowed* to speak to you," I explained. "It wasn't my choice. It's not because I'm angry with you. I am angry at Sasha, but I understand that you can't control him."

"You aren't angry?" Sophie asked.

"No. My grandparents are though. And so are the boys. But I went to see the rabbi and he said that if my grandparents told me to do something that was wrong, then I didn't have to listen."

"Really?" Sophie looked puzzled. "We would have to listen, right or wrong."

"But, he also told me," I rushed ahead, "that I couldn't shame Max by openly being your friend — it will look to everyone as if I don't mind that Sasha tried to hurt Max with a knife."

"Oh, I could kill that brother of mine," Sophie exploded. "Why does he have to do it?"

"Are you angry with me?" I asked.

Sophie shook her head. "No. I'm in almost the same circumstances. My friends don't want me to have anything to do with you. Neither does my father. He was insulted when your grandfather came and took you away."

"Did Sasha get into trouble for fighting once your father found out?" I asked.

Sophie shook her head. "I honestly think my father is more upset with your grandfather than with Sasha."

I sat down on what used to be my old bed. "The rabbi thinks we have to convince the boys to be friends."

Sophie burst out laughing. "It would be easier to convince a mad dog not to bite," she declared.

"So you believe it to be hopeless?" I grimaced.

"I do," Sophie stated.

"But even so," I persisted, "we must try. Otherwise we'll never be friends again."

"If you agree," Sophie replied, "We'll always be friends. Secret friends, but friends nevertheless."

"What good is that?" I sighed.

"It is what you wanted before — to be secret friends," Sophie reminded me.

"I know," I admitted. "But then I'll be forced to spend my time with Rachel, who is just plain mean."

"My friends aren't mean," Sophie reflected, "but they aren't best friends, either. Well, I'm willing to try if you are. I'll talk to Sasha after dinner tonight."

"And I'll talk to Max and Shmuel. Tomorrow at school, how will we tell each other what happened?"

Sophie shook her head. "I don't know."

"Write me a note," I suggested "and I'll write you a note. At recess we'll pass them to each other — as we go down the hall. It's crowded, no one should notice."

"Rachel watches you like a hawk," Sophie commented.

"True. I'll let her go ahead. I'll find a way to delay."

We shook hands on our plan and then I hurried home. Unfortunately there was no time when I could get the boys alone and I had to wait until we were all on their way to school the next morning to speak to them.

"I have something very important to discuss," I announced.

"Uh oh." Max grinned. "The fate of the world?"

"The fate of my world," I corrected him. "It's about Sasha."

"Well?" Max asked.

"Would you consider talking to him — just once — to see if the two to you could make up?"

Max snorted. "No! He attacked me with a knife. He called me a dirty Jew. Rebecca, you can't be serious."

"I *am* serious. I know what he did was terrible. But perhaps if he saw you as a human being, not some Jew to beat up, he'd stop that behaviour. Maybe he simply needs to get to know you."

"Max," Shmuel said, "Rebecca does have a point. This fighting isn't much fun. What could it hurt to talk?"

"What could it hurt?" Max repeated. "I'll tell you! He'll think we're weak. And if he senses weakness he'll be even worse."

"But Sophie is talking to him," I explained. "So he won't think you're weak. He'll know you're doing it for me, so Sophie and I can be friends again."

"You have friends," Max retorted. "You have me and Shmuel. And Fanny. And that girl, the sour looking one . . . "

"Rachel! She's awful. And I know I have you and Shmuel and don't you see that's why I won't be a friend with Sophie unless you say I can. I'd never do anything to make you look bad."

Max was quiet for a few moments after I said that. "I'll think about it," he grunted, finally. Shmuel gave me a quick wink, which Max didn't see.

"Thank you," I smiled. "Thinking is good."

When I got to school I sat at my desk and wrote a small note: *He is thinking. There is hope!* At recess I managed to pass it to Sophie in the hallway as Sophie slipped a note into my hand. I read it before going onto the playground: *He said no at first, but then, for my sake, agreed to consider it!*

After school, as usual, Rachel insisted on walking home with me. This time she walked me right to our front door. I explained that I had chores to do and escaped into the house. Fanny had just returned from school and was already peeling carrots. But when she saw me, she put them down and pulled me with her, into our sleeping room.

"*Nu,*" she said, "what on earth is happening? That was quite a speech Mama gave you the night before last." Fanny had had an important essay to write and had been at the library constantly, so we hadn't had a chance to talk.

"Sophie and I are trying to make peace between the boys," I answered.

Fanny rolled her eyes. "Well, that will happen when the sun shines at night and the moon in the morning."

"They are considering it," I protested.

"Because they are so fond of you," Fanny said. "But it won't last. Even if they declare a truce, should it hold for one day it will be a miracle!"

"What do you suggest?" I grumbled.

"You needn't sound so grumpy," Fanny admonished me. "I am simply being realistic."

"That's just another way of telling me that I have to accept things as they are," I objected. "But shouldn't I be trying to make things better?"

Fanny stared at me for a moment, thinking. "I suppose you are right, little *chachem*," she replied pensively. "The world will never improve if we accept what is and don't try for more." She sighed. "I might have suggested trying to find other friends."

"It is so difficult," I explained, "because Rachel interferes between me and the other Jewish girls."

"And don't you think *that* is worth fighting?" Fanny asked.

I was about to tell her that she didn't understand when what she said really struck me and I stopped for a moment thinking hard. It *was* worth fighting, of course, but it was so difficult, that in a way, I had put it aside as impossible.

"It is almost easier," Fanny continued, "to concentrate on changing the boys than to concentrate on changing yourself."

I knew what she meant without her explaining further. I wanted to be liked and accepted so badly that I didn't want to tackle the deep problem of Rachel, who was acting just like the Tzar of Russia.

"Fanny!" I cried. "This is unfair!"

She gave me a rueful smile. "I know. And I'm not saying that your plan with the boys is bad. Upon reflection it is worth a try. But . . . "

"Fanny, Rebecca, where are you?" It was Baba. "The carrots aren't finished . . . *oy*, I'll kill those two . . . "

Fanny and I scrambled off the bed and hurried back to the kitchen.

* * *

The next morning at school my mind was a jumble of thoughts. I *should* challenge Rachel, I knew that the minute Fanny said it, the way you simply know something is true. But how?

"Maureen," Miss MacFarland said, interrupting my thoughts. "Please come to my desk. I notice that you are scratching your head."

Reluctantly Maureen came forward as Miss MacFarland spread a piece of newspaper across her own desk. Then she pulled out her comb. I was puzzled. What was going on?

"Lice." Rachel grimaced. "Once it starts in the class it will infect everyone. Miss MacFarland is vigilant, though, and usually manages to catch the culprit before it can be spread."

"It isn't Maureen's fault," I objected. "She's hardly a 'culprit.'"

Once we had had an outbreak at our school in Oxbow. It had spread to everyone and Miss George had made us all feel dirty. I shivered. I certainly did not want to repeat that experience.

Maureen leaned over the piece of paper and Miss MacFarland carefully pulled the comb through her hair. Suddenly Miss MacFarland picked up her inkwell and brought it down with some force on the newspaper. Everyone clapped. "That's how she kills the ones that don't stick to the comb," Rachel explained. The way Rachel would probably squash me, I thought, if I tried to stand up to her. Still, I vowed that I would try the first chance I got. That chance came sooner than expected.

When recess came around Rachel, as usual, decided what we were to do. "We'll skip today," she declared. "Rebecca and Jenny will hold the rope."

"But we held the rope yesterday!" Jenny blurted out.

That was the first time I'd heard any of the girls openly defy Rachel. It suddenly occurred to me that I was probably not the only one who resented her iron hand. Maybe I could find some allies. After all, except for Clara, they had stood by me the last time I tried to stand up to Rachel. But I'd been so intimidated by Rachel, I hadn't really thought about that.

I looked at Jenny as if seeing her for the first time. She was a small girl with long curly black hair and a long thin face, and teeth that stuck out a bit like a horse's. Rachel was no prettier than Jenny, but she thought she was, and she treated Jenny the same way she treated me — as if she were beneath her in every way.

Lotty waited patiently for a decision to be made. I never heard her say an angry word and nothing seemed to upset her — yet Rachel must have bothered her or she wouldn't have defied her by offering to remain friends with me the last time I'd tried to stand up to Rachel. Deborah, who had also stuck by me last time, jumped up and down nervously, like a horse that smells a wild animal. Clara waited patiently for Rachel to decide. She was really the only one who seemed perfectly happy with things as they were.

"We did hold the rope yesterday," I said, hardly believing I was speaking the words. But my conversation with Fanny was fresh in my mind and I realized that this was as good a time as any to take a stand. "Now it's our turn to skip."

"I decide who skips when," Rachel said, a steely look coming into her eyes, "and you two will hold the rope today."

"I won't," I replied. "What about you, Jenny?"

Jenny shot me a startled glance. She took a deep breath. "I, well, I held it yesterday," she said in a tiny voice. "I should skip today."

"That is fine with me." Rachel smiled, but the smile appeared more like a grimace. "You two do not need to play with us. Give me the rope," she demanded.

I was holding the rope because Rachel had given it to me when we got to the playground. Rachel always took it from the box, and no one had ever disputed her right to take it and therefore to make all the decisions. I had a sudden picture of me running to the box at the next recess and grabbing the rope first. Then what would she do?

"No," I said, my heart pounding, "Jenny and I will skip together."

Calmly Lotty stepped forward. "There's no need," she said. "I'll hold the rope today. It's my turn."

"And so will I," Deborah blurted out, still dancing about.

I couldn't believe it. Rachel stood there with her mouth open. Was it going to be this easy? There was only her and Clara left now, two, to our four.

Rachel turned as if to leave. "That's fine," she remarked. "Clara, and I have to discuss my birthday party. Papa is taking me and my friends to The Walker Theatre."

There was a moment of silence. Even I was tempted to give in. If it hadn't been for Fanny's words, I may well have.

The Walker Theatre was too expensive for any of us to ever go to. I had heard that it was glamorous and I knew that the greatest artists performed there.

"Does anyone want to join us?"

There was another long pause and then Jenny dropped her end of the rope and walked over to join Rachel. She shrugged her shoulders a little as she glanced back over her shoulder at me.

I bit my lip. Rachel, Clara and Jenny began to walk away. Lotty, without even looking back, ran after them. That left me and Deborah.

"Want to play?" Deborah asked. Although she didn't say anything she must have found it difficult to make that choice, because her face was the colour of her flaming red hair and then she went very pale so that her freckles stood out.

I nodded. I was sweating, as if I had run all around the schoolyard three times. And my heart was skipping faster than the rope Deborah began to jump. But I felt exhilarated. I'd stood up to Rachel. And the sky hadn't fallen in. And I maybe was going to make a new friend in Deborah. She grinned at me. She didn't say anything, but I think she felt the same way I did.

When we went back to class I sat down next to Rachel as always. "Don't worry," she said to me, "I have spoken with the other girls and told them that we can't desert you. I know you've been forbidden to see Sophie, and that you are perhaps too emotional. You will still be part of our group. We won't give up on you that easily."

My heart sank. What did I have to do to break away

from her? Why did she even want to keep me in her group? I mulled that over. Perhaps letting me go would show her weakness and the other girls might then follow, as they almost had today.

There was only one thing, I thought, that would be so unacceptable to her that she would not be able to tolerate me — if I somehow could choose Sophie over her. I glanced over at Sophie, who smiled back at me.

If only the boys would see sense!

Chapter Nineteen

As we celebrated Shabbat that night, I was able to forget all about Rachel and Sophie — at least for a while. It was wonderful to be healthy again and back with my family. The men and the boys went to *shul* and we girls helped prepare dinner. When the men came home everyone gathered round the table and Baba lit the candles. The candles used to stand in her beautiful silver candlesticks, but now they were in two small chipped bowls. There used to be a white lace tablecloth, now there was no cloth at all. Baba used to dress all in white with a string of white pearls, now she wore the dark green dress she'd been wearing since the night of the fire. But it didn't matter. We still ate *gefilte* fish, followed by chicken soup, then chicken, and *tsimmes* for dessert. I wondered then whether I should leave well enough alone. I had my family. Wasn't that all that mattered? And what if Fanny was right? What if the boys made up, but the truce didn't hold? Perhaps Max would be in more danger because his guard would be down. I decided to put it all out of my mind for the moment. I would have two blissful days away from all my problems and promised myself that I would enjoy them.

When Monday morning arrived I couldn't believe how quickly the time had gone. I was dreading school, and not without cause. When I saw Sophie I wanted to tell her about the new Oz book I was reading and about *Romeo and Juliet,* but we couldn't even speak. Rachel talked on and on about her upcoming birthday, always saying how she hoped it didn't make me feel too bad since I would never have such a birthday. At the end of the day she walked me home as usual and I felt like her prisoner.

We hadn't walked far, when I noticed a crowd of young people ahead. Rachel immediately said, "Come, we'll go on the other side. Those crowds always mean a big *shemozzl.*"

But I could hear screams and yells — I had to see what was happening. Reluctantly I moved closer. It was a fight. I hoped it wasn't Max again. But it didn't seem to be the same group as usual — Max's friends against Sasha's friends. No, this was a group of Polish boys. They were big, very big and strong and there were about six of them. When I looked closer I saw that they were beating up one boy — and the boy was Sasha. And one girl, and the girl was Sophie! It was Sophie who was screaming. Sasha was doing his best to protect her, throwing himself in front of her, taking the punches for her, but he was completely outnumbered. I looked around for help. I couldn't see Max or Shmuel although they always walked home this way. I shouted at Rachel who was already on the other side of the street, "Run and get help!"

"Why should we help her?" Rachel called back. Then she ran off as fast as she could.

It took only a split second more for me to decide what to do — I couldn't leave them to fight alone and I was as tall as some of the boys, although not even a quarter as strong. I ran into the crowd screaming, "Leave them alone! Bullies. Six against two! Stop it!"

And for a minute they did stop. One of them said, "What have we here?" Another said, "A little Jew girl." "She wants to fight too, maybe?" said a third. They began jeering and then one of them, a big fellow with a scar down the side of his face, pushed me. I was terrified. Sophie caught my hand. Sasha pushed me behind him. He was bleeding from a cut on his lip and his jacket was torn on the sleeve.

"Six against three now," I sneered, trying not to let my voice crack with fear. "You're so brave!"

The boy with the scar came around behind Sasha and shoved me again. And again. My heart pounded in my ears, my cheeks burned, I felt hot and cold at the same time. Then he pushed me hard right into Sophie and we both fell over. Another boy kicked me in the leg.

I screamed, "That hurt!" I grabbed the leg that had kicked me with both hands, hard as I could, and pulled. The fellow fell down on his tush. He was furious. He lunged for me. And then suddenly I heard Max's voice.

"Hey Sasha, can't handle the Poles?" He was taunting Sasha.

"Neither can your cousin!" Sasha called back, just

before he was punched hard in the stomach, and he doubled over. I was punched hard on the arm and the back by the one who was still on the ground.

"Max!" I screamed. "Help!"

"Rebecca?" And then I heard him whistle — the whistle he used to bring his gang together — and in a moment all the Jewish boys were there fighting, with Sasha, against the Poles. Sophie and I crawled away, clinging on to each other. It was a long, mean fight, but finally the Polish boys had had enough and one by one they staggered away.

Max and Shmuel ran over to me. Sasha ran over to Sophie. At the same time they all said, "Are you all right?"

We looked up and smiled.

"We will be," I replied, knowing that this was a moment I couldn't let slip away, "if you and Sasha shake hands."

Max and Sasha eyed each other. They had fought well together.

"I'll shake hands," Max said, "if Sasha takes back the things he's called me. In front of everyone."

The other Jewish boys began to gather round them.

Sasha's face went red.

"Sasha!" Sophie scolded him, getting up, "I know you don't mean those things. And these boys just saved us."

Sasha grimaced. Finally, after what seemed to be an endless pause he said, "I take it back," and put out his hand.

Max extended his. Then Shmuel. The other boys nodded as if witnessing a treaty being signed.

"Step one," I said to Sophie, smiling.

* * *

Step two became Rabbi Kahanovitch's problem after I ran to the *shul* to catch him just before services to report my success.

Nothing happened right away. But three days later at dinner, Baba, who was hovering around the table as usual instead of sitting, said, "I understand, Max, you have made up with this boy, Sasha."

The rabbi must have been here, I thought, holding my breath for what Baba would say next.

"Yes, Mama," Max answered.

"That's good. Better for your studies than fighting. Rebecca, you may now speak to the sister."

"Thank you, Baba!" I exclaimed.

Fanny gave me a little wink.

"And don't be finding someone new to fight with!" Baba instructed Max.

"Who, me?" he said innocently.

I had to bite my tongue to keep from laughing.

At that moment life seemed almost perfect to me. I was back with my family and I had a best friend. My only other wish was to move into an apartment with Papa, Mama, Sol, and Leah. Papa had started work at the Walker, so maybe that wasn't too far off.

I thought about going to school the next morning. Who knew how long the truce between Sasha and Max would last? And what about Rachel? She would be furious that I had gone back to Sophie, which in one way was good, as she'd probably finally give up on me. But there was no doubt she would try to make my life miserable. She'd try to convince at least some of the girls to be mean to me, that was certain. But I had come to realize that being liked by everyone didn't matter. Sophie liked me and that did matter.

I thought back to the conversation I'd had with Masha before I left Oxbow. I'd been afraid no one in Winnipeg would like me. And in a way, Rachel had almost made my worst fear come true. But, much to my own surprise, I'd chosen one good friend over everything.

Well, life was full of surprises, I'd certainly learned that. Nothing was forever, everything could change in a second — except, perhaps, the way people you loved felt about you and the way you felt about them. That was something that I *could* count on. Life was wonderful, wasn't it?

"Let us in on the joke," Shmuel said, as he saw me smiling to myself over my soup.

"Everything," I replied. "The whole *mish-mosh* of life."

"It may be a *mish-mosh,*" Zaida said, "but at least it's our *mish-mosh,* eh, Rebecca?"

"Yes Zaida," I smiled. And I went back to eating Baba's barley soup.

Carol Matas is the author of more than two dozen best-selling books for children and young adults, and is best known for her historical novels, including *Daniel's Story, After the War, Greater than Angels, Sworn Enemies, Lisa,* and *Jesper.* She also writes contemporary fiction, as well as fantasy novels with co-author Perry Nodelman.

Carol's books have won many honours, including two Governor General's Award nominations, the Silver Birch Award and the Red Maple Award. She lives in Winnipeg, Manitoba.